THE ORCHARD BOOK OF
Stories from the Ballet

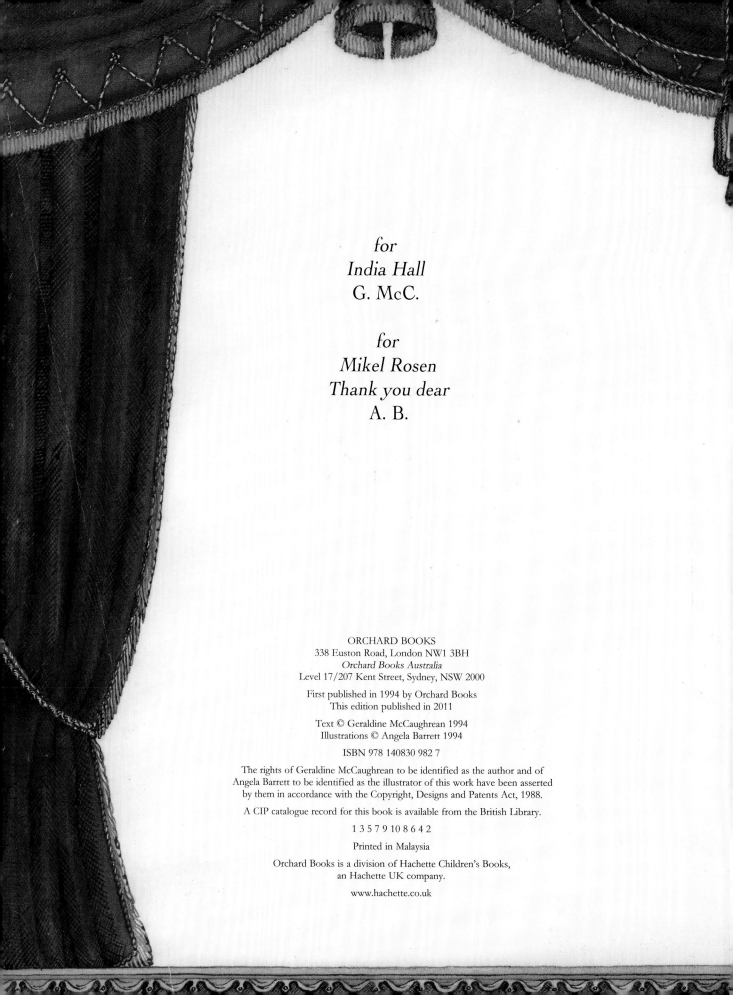

for
India Hall
G. McC.

for
Mikel Rosen
Thank you dear
A. B.

ORCHARD BOOKS
338 Euston Road, London NW1 3BH
Orchard Books Australia
Level 17/207 Kent Street, Sydney, NSW 2000

First published in 1994 by Orchard Books
This edition published in 2011

Text © Geraldine McCaughrean 1994
Illustrations © Angela Barrett 1994

ISBN 978 140830 982 7

The rights of Geraldine McCaughrean to be identified as the author and of
Angela Barrett to be identified as the illustrator of this work have been asserted
by them in accordance with the Copyright, Designs and Patents Act, 1988.

A CIP catalogue record for this book is available from the British Library.

1 3 5 7 9 10 8 6 4 2

Printed in Malaysia

Orchard Books is a division of Hachette Children's Books,
an Hachette UK company.

www.hachette.co.uk

THE ORCHARD BOOK OF

Stories from the Ballet

GERALDINE McCAUGHREAN  ANGELA BARRETT

ORCHARD

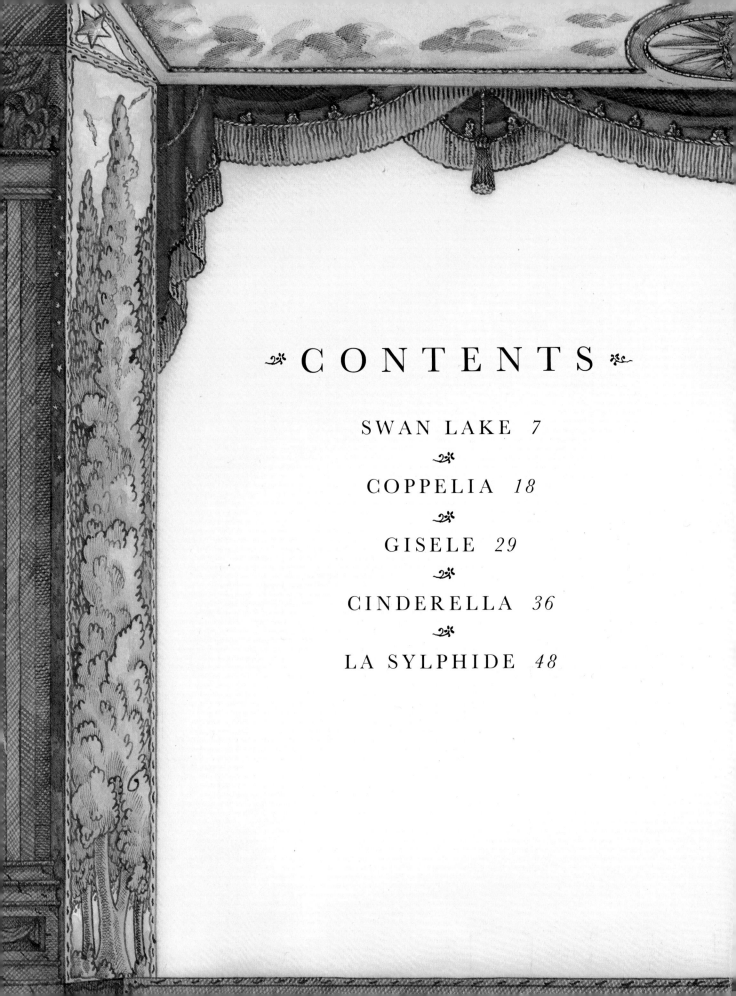

·❧ CONTENTS ❧·

SWAN LAKE

A Prince's birthday! Days of celebration! Feasting! Presents!
Dancing! Heralds carried the invitation far and wide: "Come to
the Royal Castle tomorrow, for Prince Siegfried is twenty-one
years old and will soon take his rightful place as King!"

Already the castle gardens were crowded with people from the
village, all come to wish Prince Siegfried happy birthday with
flowers and dancing.

"There! There he is!" they cheered. "Oh, isn't he handsome!
Imagine being *married* to someone as handsome as that!"

"I wonder who he'll choose for a wife!"

"The Prince? Marry? He'd sooner go hunting with his friends."

It was true. Siegfried's mother, the Queen, was quite upset

about it. She knew how much he liked hunting: she even gave him a crossbow for his birthday present. But she also knew it was time for the Prince to be choosing a wife, marrying, having sons and daughters of his own. She often spoke to him about it. She even invited beautiful princesses to the castle. But Siegfried never paid them any attention. He just rode off into the forests with his friends, and left the princesses taking tea with the Queen. "*Really*, Siegfried, parties are all very well," his mother said, "but you must start taking life more seriously. You must choose a bride. Tell him, Wolfgang. You're his teacher. Tell him how important it is!" Away went the Queen, but the Prince had hardly heard a word she said. He was too busy admiring his new crossbow.

"Your excellent mother is quite right, young man," said old Wolfgang sternly. "There are some things far more important than parties. Be a good boy. Choose a nice, pretty girl at the ball tomorrow and settle down."

But Siegfried had hardly heard a word his teacher said. He was too busy watching a skein of swans flying across the sky. "Swans! Come on everybody! Let's practise our shooting!" cried the Prince. "With any luck there'll be something better than princesses at the ball tomorrow: there'll be roast swan!"

All the young huntsmen set off together for the wood. But in among the trees, searching for the swans, they were soon

separated. Siegfried found himself alone beside a lake. The flock of swans had landed on the water and were swimming towards the bank. They paddled ashore on their large black feet, all the little cygnets flurrying out together. Last to come was the whitest swan of all, wearing – could it be? – *a golden crown*. Siegfried laid an arrow to his bow.

That was when he saw it: that most wonderful of sights. The milk-white swan spread its wide wings, stretched its long neck high in the air, and the feathers, the great black feet, the orange beak, the wings – all but the crown – melted away like snow. There stood a beautiful woman, lifting a gown of white above her knees as she waded ashore. Next moment all the other swans were transformed into young women, the cygnets into little children. Siegfried's crossbow dropped from his hands and the noise startled them.

"Don't be afraid!" he exclaimed in a whisper. "Am I dreaming? Tell me, who are you?"

The girl in the crown looked about her with shining black eyes. "It's dangerous. Von Rothbart will be watching. He's always watching!" But Siegfried would not leave until he had heard her whole unhappy story.

The swan-maiden's name was Odette – Princess Odette – her kingdom a land far, far away. She and her ladies-in-waiting, even their little children, were prisoners of a terrible magic. And who but the sorcerer von Rothbart could have cast a spell so wicked over such a princess? She and all the swan-maidens were doomed by a terrible curse:

Flap and fly
In the weary sky;
By day a swan
With feathers wan;
Only at night
The lovely sight
Which once I swore
Would never more
Offend my sight
With goodness bright.
The world will soon forget
Princess Odette!

Even at night, when they wore human shape, the evil von Rothbart kept watch over his prisoners, disguised as an owl, yellow eyes watching, watching, watching.

"Can nothing save you?" cried Prince Siegfried. All night he had sat and listened to her story.

"Nothing but love," she said sadly.

"Oh, then you're saved!" It was true: Siegfried had loved her ever since the first moment he saw her black eyes shine. All night his love had been growing. "*I love you!*" he exclaimed.

"Oh, but you would have to swear to love me for ever. Nothing less can break a spell!"

"I'll do it!" he cried, without a moment's thought.

But daylight was already creeping through the trees. Odette pulled away from him, drawn by magic back into the lake. Her arms began to stiffen into fronded wings.

"Come to the castle tomorrow!" called Siegfried. "To the birthday ball! Come, and I'll choose you for my wife!"

Somewhere an owl hooted, a terrible, dismal sound. A milk-white swan gliding out over the lake nodded her lovely head.

"Does he think he can break my spell so easily?" Von Rothbart hooted with laughter, and his daughter laughed too.

His spiteful, spoiled, ugly daughter Odile laughed a quacking laugh. "So you won't let her marry him?" Odile had wanted the handsome Prince for many years and hated Odette for winning his love.

"No, no. *You* shall have that honour," said the sorcerer. "Tonight I shall mask you in magic and dress you in disguise. I'll give you the face of Odette. You shall dance the night away while Siegfried swears away his love for ever!" Again he hooted with laughter, just like an owl.

That night, at the castle, the air glistened with ribbons and silk. Princesses with hair of yellow and black and brown arrived in coaches of gold and silver and glass to smile at Prince Siegfried and wish him happy birthday. (What they really wished was to marry him, of course.)

"Meet Princess Zoë," said the Queen.

"Meet Princess Chloë.

"Meet Princess Clothilda.

"Meet Princess Matilda.

"Meet Princess Mariana," said the Queen. "Meet Princess Tatiana!"

But Siegfried only looked over their shoulders, watching the door, waiting for Odette to arrive.

There! A woman dressed all in scarlet swept into the ballroom, lifted her veil and – yes! There were Odette's black eyes, Odette's white skin, Odette's sweet red mouth. Siegfried rushed to take her in his arms, and the dancing began. Apart from the Princesses, the guests were amazed and delighted to see such a change in the Prince.

But he should have looked more deeply into those black eyes.

"Now you may swear that you love me," said Odile.

"Oh, I do! I swear it!"

With a noise like a heart breaking, a pane of glass broke in the tall castle windows. There, battering against the glass with wide, white wings, pecking at the glass with an orange beak, kicking at the glass with large black feet, was a milk-white swan.

Odette flung herself against the window so hard that it burst open. But a guest at the party, a man with large yellow eyes, slammed the window shut again with a hooting laugh.

"For ever and a day. Swear!" said Odile.

"For ever and a day!" vowed Siegfried.

"And so you have chosen your wife," declared von Rothbart. "Sworn undying love to my dear daughter, Odile."

"*Odile?*"

"Congratulations, my dear son-in-law."

Siegfried looked up then and caught sight of von Rothbart and, beyond him, clamouring against the glass, the ragged, haggard shape of a swan.

"Come, Odile!" said her father. "We have what we came for!"

"Never!" cried the Prince. But as he drew his sword and rushed towards the sorcerer, the room filled with smoke and thunder.

"What? Do you think a puny sword can destroy an evil the like of mine?" cried von Rothbart.

A howling wind blew open all the windows. And away across a black and thundery sky, a swan was swept by the magician's stormy laughter, over the treetops, towards the lake.

The day ended. The sun sank and returned Odette to human shape. But it took with it all her hopes and dreams. When her friends saw her coming through the woods, her hair wild, her gown torn, her hands bruised with banging on the window's glass, they knew that Siegfried had not broken the spell. They were doomed for ever to be swans by day, maidens by night.

"He forgot me! He forgot me! So soon he forgot me! He danced with Odile! He swore to love Odile! He chose Odile to be his wife!" She rushed past them to the shore of the lake and was about to throw herself into the water.

"Wait! Princess! What are you doing?" The swan-maidens thought she must have forgotten that she was not a swimming swan.

"I can't wait! If I'm going to drown myself, I must do it while I'm in human form!"

"Drown yourself? No!" Her friends pulled her away from the water, but they could do nothing to comfort her.

"I'll find her! I'll explain! I was tricked! My vow means nothing!" wailed Prince Siegfried as he raced through the rainy woods.

Rain, sleet, snow. The wind howled and the trees crashed down around him. Von Rothbart's magic was at work, trying to stop the Prince from reaching Odette. But he fought his way past the lashing branches, he bent his head into the driving rain and he stumbled on towards the lake. "Odette! I'm sorry! Odette! Forgive me!"

She heard him coming. She would have run away, but he caught her up in his arms. "Forgive me, Odette! I was tricked by that villain Rothbart. He tricked me with magic. He blinded me, so that I couldn't see you until it was too late. But he can't blind

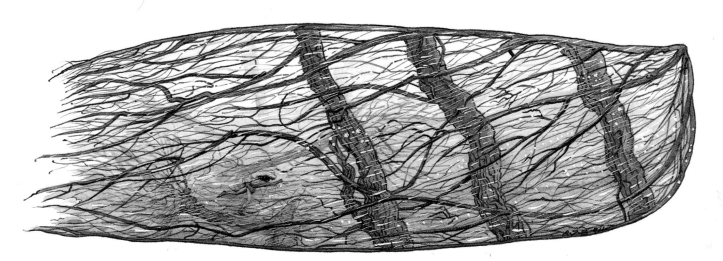

me to the truth. It's you I love, not Odile. It's you I shall love for ever!"

She forgave him, of course she did. But she did so sadly, with eyes full of tears. "I love you too, Siegfried, but nothing can undo what's done. Your promise is made, and I and my ladies will be prisoners for ever, swans by day and women by night. And Odile shall be your queen."

"That's right!" cried von Rothbart appearing in a clap of thunder, with a laugh like lightning. "My prisoners always, in a land where my daughter is Queen! You! Swan-maidens! Dawn is coming. Get back to your lake now. Preen your white feathers and waddle on your black feet, and eat weed as I taught you!" The swan-maidens fled, sobbing with terror.

But Odette clung to the Prince. "Oh, Siegfried! I wish you had shot me with your crossbow that first time you saw me! Life will be nothing without you!"

"You're right," whispered Siegfried. "But why live apart when we can die together?"

Von Rothbart heard them. The words struck terror into his wicked soul. "No!" he begged. "NO!"

But they did not hear him. Princess Odette and Prince Siegfried were looking into each other's eyes as they plunged into the lake and the chilly waters closed over them.

In that moment, all von Rothbart's magic burst inside him, scalding, freezing, poisonous, deadly. He fell dead on the spot.

The swan-maidens, and their frightened little cygnets, found themselves ankle-deep in water, surrounded by fallen feathers. The spell was broken.

Dawn rose over the lake: sunlight danced on the water. And there, in a magical world of light, somewhere between Earth and Sky, Prince Siegfried and Princess Odette danced too, together for ever, forever dancing for joy. Their love had been far too great for Death to hold prisoner. They simply slipped out of its grasp, to live together in a world of never-ending happiness.

C O P P E L I A

Everybody was talking about the Duke's present: a new bell to
hang in the town hall, spilling its music down over the town. Such
a generous gift! And now, to mark the event, the Mayor was
offering a bag of gold to every boy and girl to marry on the day
the bell first rang. "Who will take up my offer?" he bellowed in
the town square, holding up the gold for everyone to see.

"Swanhilda and Franz! They will, for sure!"

"Oh yes, Swanhilda and Franz! They're made for each other!"

"Here they come! Love's young dream!"

Franz grinned and Swanhilda blushed a charming red, cooling
her cheek against Franz's sleeve. Then, to turn the attention away
from her, she joked, "What about Old Coppelius? He's got a little
girlfriend, haven't you seen?"

"Doctor Coppelius? Ha ha ha! That's a good one! Oohoo-hoo!"

The town's laughter washed up against the Doctor's tall, thin house, over the balcony, through the closed shutters and into that dark room where the old man both lived and worked. He heard the laughter. But he was used to it. What people don't understand, they laugh at. And the young always laugh at the old. For all their nosy prying, nobody knew a thing about Coppelius, or what he got up to in that tall, thin house of his, behind closed shutters. His dismal black clothes frightened his neighbours; his horrible temper kept them at bay. So no one had dared ask him to his face just who the pretty girl was, sitting on his balcony reading a book. A visitor? A relation? He smiled with pleasure at their ignorance, and at his delicious, delectable secret.

The girl certainly caused a stir among the young men. When Franz saw her, he could hardly take his eyes off her. He waved. He called out, "Good day!" But the girl only went on reading.

"She's not interested in *you*," said Swanhilda angrily, "though anyone can see what you think of her. More than you think of me, that's for sure!" And she stamped her foot and burst into tears. Unfortunately Franz was too busy staring up at the pretty girl even to notice.

"Perhaps they won't be getting a bag of gold from the Mayor after all," said the people in the square. "It looks as if Franz has seen a girl he prefers to Swanhilda."

At the end of the afternoon Doctor Coppelius came and fetched the girl indoors. Young couples from all over town were dancing in the marketplace, but she did not come and join in. Nor did Swanhilda, who was sulking. But Franz was there, enjoying himself with his friends, drinking a little bit more than he should.

Old Coppelius locked his front door with a big brass key and went out to buy supper. The music jarred his thoughts and upset the calculations he was making in his head. The dancers in the street deliberately bumped and barged into him. "Young people! Bah!" he grumbled. "No courtesy or respect, any of you!" And of course that made the boys behave even worse. They jostled and shouldered him, spun him round and tripped him up, even made him drop his key. Franz was one of them. Swanhilda would never have let him do it. But Franz seemed to have forgotten Swanhilda.

She came along soon after, with a crowd of girls, complaining bitterly about men in general and Franz in particular. Then she caught sight of something shining in the gutter. "A key?"

"So big, too!"

"Looks like the key to a fortress!"

"It was lying outside the Doctor's door. I bet it's his!" said Swanhilda. And bold as brass she turned the key in the door. "There! What did I tell you?"

"You're never going inside!" cried her friends.

"Why not? Nobody's home. We saw Coppelius just now, going into the café."

"What about the pretty girl?"

"She'll be in bed – or out dancing. Come on! A quick peep won't hurt."

"Ooh, Swanhilda, you are brave!"

Nervous, giggling, egging each other on, the girls climbed the stairs. A light was still burning in that mysterious upper room. Swanhilda led the way into a big workshop and they stared about

them, open-mouthed. "Well! Who'd have thought it? Old Coppelius a toy maker!"

From floor to ceiling, wall to wall, and hanging from the rafters were a hundred different toys: clockwork mice, stiff stick puppets and floppy dolls, jacks-in-boxes, hens and foxes, cuckoo clocks and crowing cocks . . . And a long row of big willow baskets.

"Clockwork toys!" exclaimed Swanhilda. "These are *clock-work*!"

So they turned keys, they flicked switches; they squealed with joy and fright as the whole room came to life. Clockwork soldiers marched up and down, cats scurried around their feet, fairies twirled and birds trilled. It was pandemonium – but far too thrilling to stop. That's how mischief is, once it takes a hold.

Swanhilda looked in one of the baskets and jumped back – first with a cry of fright, then with a shriek of laughter. "Look!" she cried, pulling out a hank of hair. "Here's Coppelius's little girlfriend! Here's the girl Franz couldn't take his eyes off! She's just a puppet! What a joke! Fine couple they'd make, wouldn't they? A pair of woodenheads!"

The girls were so busy laughing that they almost missed the scuff-scuff-scuff of something heavy being dragged along the street, the clang of the balcony rail, the rattle of something up against the window.

"Look out! What's that noise? Someone's coming!"

"Quick!"

"Run!"

"Hide!"

"Let's get out of here!"

"The Doctor!"

The girls scattered in panic.

It was not old Coppelius coming. It was Franz!

He had brought a ladder to climb up to the lighted window and find out for himself just who the pretty girl was who had refused to wave to him or answer his greetings.

In he climbed, into the Doctor's wonderful workshop. He was just as amazed as the girls had been to see all the toys Coppelius had made. He wandered in a daze from perch to cage, from cuckoo clock to jack-in-a-box, though he did not find the girl he had come in search of . . . nor Swanhilda curled up in hiding not five steps away.

Deep in thought, weary, the old Doctor leaned heavily on his stick as he hobbled home from supper. All these years he had dreamed his dream: while he ate, while he worked, while he lay on his hard bed and failed to sleep. Little by little his dream had taken him over, possessed him, blinded him to every other joy. People might think he was a sour old hermit, but deep inside he felt a great happiness coming. Coppelia was finished! He had lavished his greatest skill and best materials making her. While carving that pretty face, he had found himself whispering to it, stroking it, loving it, almost. All that remained was to bring his little lady to life, and a conjuror had told him the very way to do it. The Doctor's hand shook on the head of his walking cane. Had the conjuror been telling the truth? Would it really work? And where was that last vital ingredient to come from which would transform Coppelia into a living, breathing woman: the tender wife that Coppelius had never had.

What's this? My door unlocked? he thought. Thieves in among my toys? Burglars, and my sweet Coppelia all alone? His fright and his temper mounting, the Doctor tap-tapped his way up the stairs and burst into his workshop.

He caught Franz red-handed. "Aha! A robber! I ought to thrash you and turn you over to the police!" he cried, brandishing his walking stick, driving Franz backwards into a corner. "Shall I do that? Shall I?"

"Please, sir, I didn't . . . I mean, I was only . . ."

"No! You're right. I won't," declared Coppelius, to Franz's even greater astonisment. "Don't get nearly enough visitors. What am I but a lonely old man? No friends. Nobody to drink coffee with. How good to see a young face! Pull up a chair. Sit down. Make yourself at home, young . . ."

"F-F-F-Franz, s-s-sir." Hardly able to believe his luck, Franz sat down and drank the coffee that Coppelius brought him on a battered old tray. He drank, he nodded, he fell asleep. Drinking that coffee was his big mistake.

"Now's my chance!" crowed Coppelius. "All these years I've waited! All these weeks I've puzzled my brains where I might find the last ingredients. Now this worthless young lout comes of his own accord, breaks in, roots about among my belongings! It's an omen – a godsend! His life force can bring my beautiful doll to life! At last! My Coppelia! Where are you, my darling girl?"

He lay Franz, drugged and sleeping, on top of the basket where he kept his pretty masterpiece. Then, with an evil-smelling alchemy, spark-crackling chemistry, and mumbled magic, he cast his wicked spell.

Rolling Franz aside, as floppy as a doll, he flung open the basket. *"Now live, my Coppelia!"* he cried.

And lo and behold! Up rose the doll from the basket – as pretty as any princess – and began to dance. At first she was a little stiff, as you would expect a puppet to be, then more and more supple, more and more lithe. She danced as though she knew every dance in the world. And once she had started, there was no stopping her. She whirled the Doctor around till he was dizzy, and when she saw Franz, she shook him too, as if she wanted to dance him back to life.

And lo and behold! Franz began to groan and get up, to stir and to stagger about.

"Oh, my beautiful Coppelia!"

The doll spun round, but the Doctor was not talking to her. He had just found the body of his pretty puppet in a cupboard, wig gone, dress stripped off. "Who did this to you? And if you are here . . . *WHO IS THAT*?"

"It's Swanhilda, you wicked old wizard!" cried Franz with a laugh. "My lovely, clever little Swanhilda playing a trick on you!"

"Thought you could steal my Franz's life force and bring your silly doll to life, did you, you old rascal?" jeered Swanhilda, taking off the doll's wig. "Well it serves you right if the whole town is laughing at you tomorrow!"

But Old Coppelius could only hug his broken, spoiled puppet and sob, "Coppelia! What, not alive? Poor Coppelia! What have they done to you, my dear, dear girl?"

After such a fright, Franz was a changed boy. He never wanted to look at another girl. Besides, he admired Swanhilda so much for the trick she had played on Coppelius that he wanted to marry her then and there.

So the whole town *was* laughing next day, laughing with delight at the news that Franz and Swanhilda were to be married and have the Mayor's bag of gold for a wedding present.

They laughed at the Old Doctor, too, as he stumbled down his steps and across the town square, seeing nothing but the cobbles at his feet. Many of his toys had been broken by the girls' careless meddling. And his dreams of bringing a puppet to life were gone for ever. "Vandals! Thieves! Hooligans!" he spat at the knots of youths and girls who jigged about in their Sunday best, giggling behind their hands. "Is that what a man's life is worth to you – five minutes' laughter?"

"Not at all! You shall have the bag of gold," said Franz generously. "I've got all the gold I need in my priceless Swanhilda. Today everyone should be happy! Everyone in the world!" And the new bell in the town hall tower started to ring, spilling its happy music over the whole town.

But the gold in the bag was not as bright as Coppelia's hair, nor as warm as the cheek which had pressed against his while Old Coppelius believed himself to be dancing with her. There are some things that money cannot buy.

GISELE

Beware! The depths of the forest and the shores of its bitter lake are haunted. Don't go there after midnight, or you may see the wylies dancing. And if you see them, it may be the last sight you ever see. For the dance of the wylies is not for the eyes of the living.

These spirits – each one the ghost of a young girl – all suffered the same fate when they were alive: to be loved by a faithless man, promised marriage by him, and spurned before the wedding day. Their hearts broken in life, they leap from their over-early graves to dance from midnight till dawn, seizing what lonely happiness they can in the moonlight.

One night, Queen Myrtha, guardian and ruler over the wylies, had a new spirit to introduce to her company of ghosts. "Greet

Gisèle, ladies, who loved a prince and was deceived by him."

A patch of freshly dug soil stirred, heaved, and out of her grave stepped Gisèle, veiled and dressed in gauzy white as all wylies are. She looked about her with empty, tragic eyes. "Tell us your story, Gisèle," said the Queen with a grim smile. The other wylies pressed closer, hungry always for the companionship of another unhappy girl with a history like their own.

"Two men loved me," said Gisèle flatly. "First Hilarion the gamekeeper and then . . . and then . . ."

"Prince Albrecht, was it not?" the Queen prompted heartlessly.

"He did not tell me he was a prince. He said he was a peasant. He did not tell me he was engaged to the Princess Bathilde. He only told me that he loved me with all his heart and soul."

The wylies groaned a low, unearthly groan that set the leaves shaking and the owls clawing at the boughs overhead.

"Hilarion was jealous," Gisèle went on. "He wanted to win me back, I suppose. So he took great joy in telling me the truth. He even brought me Albrecht's golden sword, told me how he'd lied. My Albrecht. My fiancé. My love."

The wylies sighed such a sigh that the brown and rotting leaves rolled over on the forest floor.

"I asked Albrecht if what Hilarion said was true. He couldn't deny it. Two fiancées. Two loves. Two lies." Gisèle passed a hand in front of her face, remembering. "I think I lost my mind then, because I started to dance, right there in the village street, though Mama begged me to stop, and so did Hilarion and Albrecht, my love . . . I danced and I danced, although my heart has always been weak. Suddenly a pain in my chest – no breath to dance, no strength to take another step! I know I must have died, for here I am, among the wylies. When I was little, Mama talked about you often in her bedtime stories. But I never thought to be one, no never, God help me."

That made the Queen angry, because she liked to think of her subjects as happy and fortunate. "Just think what a lucky escape you've had, girl! To be free of those vile *men*; to dance where no foul, graceless *man* may come and interrupt your dancing." Queen Myrtha, too, had been betrayed by her lover, and hated all men with a deep, immortal loathing. If one strayed through the forest at night and happened to glimpse the gauzy white figures dancing, he never lived to see morning. Such was the Queen's hatred.

Just then there was indeed a rustle of leaves, a cracking of twigs. Someone was coming! At once the Queen commanded her ghostly subjects to follow her, and she hurried deeper into the forest rather than be seen by a living person. Gisèle did not follow, however, but hung back. And so, from a hiding place in the corner of the glade, she saw Prince Albrecht bring a spray of flowers to her grave.

He was distracted with misery. His shoulders heaved with sobs, and he rocked to and fro as he knelt praying. "Forgive me, little Gisèle," he whispered. "What have I done? I truly loved you, little girl. For all my disguises and my lies. For all my parents betrothed me to the Princess Bathilde and I ought to have loved her. Once I'd seen you, how could I love anyone else? Oh, dearest! They would never have let a prince marry a country girl, but God knows, that was all I ever wanted!"

Gisèle crept up behind him and tapped teasingly on his shoulder. He turned with a start, but saw no one. She covered his eyes with her hands and whispered, "Guess who!" and he stumbled to his feet in a daze of horror and joy and tried to catch hold of her. She was too quick for him. Darting and leaping playfully ahead of him, she led him out of the glade in a helter-skelter dash between the dapple-barked birches. Laughing and coaxing, she lured him on. But though her manner was playful, her purpose was deadly serious. If Queen Myrtha were to see him, Albrecht would never be allowed to leave the forest alive. To save his life, Gisèle led him as far as possible, out of harm's way. All her bitterness was gone and she wanted only to save him from the vengeance of the wylies.

No one was there, in the glade, to take such pity on Hilarion the gamekeeper. When he came searching for the grave of his lifelong love, he found nothing but an open, empty pit. And when he looked up from his grief, he found himself surrounded by ghostly white forms. The wylies' golden hair spread on the air like a poacher's net, and their arms encircled his throat like the poacher's snare. They drove him to the brink of the lake, hounded him to where the soil crumbled from under his boots into the deep water below.

"Stop! I never betrayed a woman!" he protested. "I tried to warn Gisèle, that's all! I tried to warn her against that deceiver, Albrecht!" But the wylies allowed no difference between one man and another, hating them all.

They forced him over the edge. With a single cry, the devoted, faithful Hilarion, whose jealousy had broken his own beloved's heart, fell to his death in the cold water.

"I spy another stranger!" cried the Queen, and, despite Gisèle's efforts, the wylies crowded round Albrecht and her like seagulls mobbing wrens. Just as with Hilarion, they started to drive Albrecht towards the lake, to drown him.

"No! Don't! Pity him, please!" begged Gisèle.

"As much as we pity all of his kind," spat the Queen venomously. And seeing rebellion in Gisèle's shineless eyes, she pronounced a sentence all the more spiteful on Prince Albrecht. "You shall *dance* him to death!" she told Gisèle, and with a wave of her magic wand forced the girl to begin dancing.

Albrecht was spellbound by her movements. He had to dance with her; he could not help himself. It was a wild, demonic dance, which gave no pause for breath. After three hours it had wearied both dancers to the point of collapse. But Gisèle's weak heart no longer beat in her chest; she could not die a second time. When Albrecht fell choking, soaked in sweat and with the blood hammering in his temples, Gisèle made herself dance on, circling him, shielding him from the malice of the spirits while he recovered his breath. Then the Queen's magic forced him to his feet once more.

"Pity him! Spare him! I still love him!" cried Gisèle as she danced.

But the words only incensed Myrtha. "Let him die, an example to all the rest of his kind!"

"What do I care?" gasped Albrecht, his legs starting to fail him. "I don't want to live in a world without you, Gisèle!" It seemed as if the Dance of Death was about to claim another victim.

Then suddenly a cock crew in some distant farmyard, and the morning star glimmered and went out in the eastern sky. A church bell began to ring. A new day had begun, and the wylies were powerless to stay. Each one, including the Queen, was drawn irresistibly to her grave, as if to a soft, safe bed. Gisèle had danced the night away and, with it, Albrecht's sentence of death.

Though the Prince was left with nothing but empty air in his weary embrace, still he had the knowledge that Gisèle had forgiven him his lies and still returned – would always return – his love, even from beyond the grave. He knelt in the dappled morning light and wept until the sun was high in the sky.

CINDERELLA

"Cinderella! That's what we'll call you. Cinderella! Because you're always sitting warming your feet in the cinders instead of working! Lazy, idle, good-for-nothing Cinderella!"

Once upon a time those were the squeaks and squawks that flew about in the big house on the hill. Three sisters lived there with their father, but you would have thought there were only two sisters and one scullery maid, for the two older ones, Gouda and Gorgonzola, treated the youngest with such dreadful unkindness. "Only a *step*sister," they said. "Hardly a sister at all." And they made her do all the housework and fetch and carry for them without ever a word of thanks in return.

One day there was even more work than usual. There was to be a Royal Ball at the palace. The King wished his son, the Prince, to meet every lady of noble birth and from among them choose a wife! That is why Gouda and Gorgonzola had been trying on different dresses and hats all morning, strutting vainly up and down in front of the mirror. The effort quite wore them out. They had only enough energy left to bully Cinderella and quarrel between themselves. She could hear them overhead in the warm living room. Cinderella sighed a deep sigh.

A voice behind her said, "Listen to them! Hammer and tongs. I wish they wouldn't."

"Father! I didn't hear you come in!" Cinderella ran to get her father some tea and he sat by the kitchen fire to drink it.

"I wish they wouldn't be so unkind to you, my dear," he said. Cinderella smiled. "I wish things could be as they were in the old days: just you, your mother and I."

Cinderella might have asked then why he did not stand up to his stepdaughters, why he let them behave so badly. Her father was not the bravest of men, but she loved him very much. "There, there, don't fret, Father," she said, and patted his shoulder with one hand while she stirred the soup for lunch with the other. She had long ago realised there was no one in the world to save her from Gouda and Gorgonzola.

"Cinderella! The door! Do you expect us to get up and answer the door ourselves?" Gouda bawled down the stairs.

It was the dressmaker with more lace.

"*Cinderella, the door!*"

It was the milliner, with new hats.

"*Cinderella, the door!*"

It was the dancing master to teach the stepsisters the latest dances in time for the Royal Ball.

"*Cinderella, the door!*"

It was the coach, come to take Gouda and Gorgonzola and their father to the Royal Palace. The door closed one last time, and the house fell silent. Cinderella sat down, put her face in her hands and cried and cried as if her heart would break.

"So you wanted to go too, did you?"

Cinderella turned round with a start and the sewing box slipped out of her lap, spilling its contents across the kitchen floor. She was a little afraid to think that a stranger – an old beggarwoman – had found her way into the house uninvited.

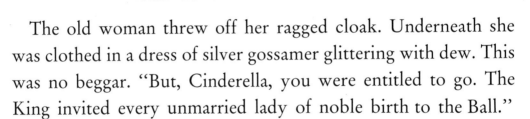

The old woman threw off her ragged cloak. Underneath she was clothed in a dress of silver gossamer glittering with dew. This was no beggar. "But, Cinderella, you were entitled to go. The King invited every unmarried lady of noble birth to the Ball."

"Ah yes, but I don't really count as a lady any more. Anyway, how did you know I was . . .?"

"Oh, but I do, Cinderella. I know everything about you: your goodness and patience and all your heart's desires. You see, I am your Fairy Godmother, and I am here to make sure that your dreams come true."

Then visitors began to arrive for Cinderella: not hairdressers or jewellers or dressmakers, but *Fairies*! Yes, Fairies from the Land of Dewfall. One brought her a spray of flowers bright as spring. One brought her lizards green as summer. One brought her a pumpkin golden as autumn, and one brought her six mice as white as winter. Strange presents, but when nobody has ever given you so much as a kind word, even a lizard can seem a marvellous gift.

Then her Fairy Godmother touched each present with a magic wand, and all at once the mice were turned into prancing horses, the pumpkin into a coach of coppery splendour, the lizards into coachmen. "You *shall* go to the Royal Ball, Cinderella," said her Fairy Godmother.

"Oh, but will they let me in? Don't you think it would be a rudeness to the Prince if I went in these rags?"

Her Godmother laughed, and touched the spray of spring blossoms with her wand. Then all at once Cinderella found herself dressed in cream silk and silver satin, a diamond tiara and snowy gloves. And on her tiny feet was a pair of glass slippers.

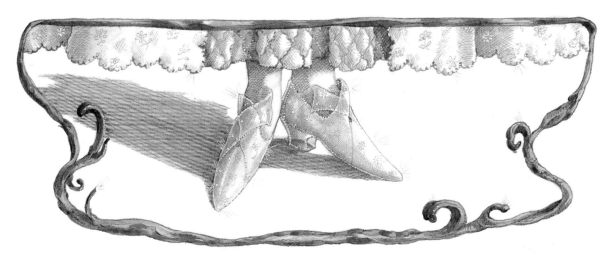

"Listen hard and listen well, Godchild," said her Godmother sternly. "My magic cannot hold past midnight. When the clock strikes twelve, everything will turn back into what it was."

Midnight. It seemed a lifetime away. Ahead lay the whole evening, a magical evening. The Fairies of the Four Seasons fanned her burning cheeks with their wings, and the night sky seemed to be full of stars, all swooping low to gaze at Cinderella's loveliness and to escort her on her way.

Of course she was late. Her sisters and father had long since arrived, and the dancing had begun. A fanfare of trumpets announced the Prince, and all eyes turned to see the plush scarlet tunic, the dashing run down the grand stairway, the circlet of gold crowning the royal head. Not a lady saw him but her heart beat faster and her fan fluttered with excitement.

But who could this be now? The trumpets were announcing a latecomer. What bad manners to arrive after the Prince!

At the head of the staircase stood a princess – yes, a princess surely! The room caught its breath. The dance music faltered to a silence.

"Who *is* she?"

". . . must come from far away . . ."

". . . a foreign princess . . ."

". . . or we would have heard tell before now of such a beauty!"

The Prince looked back up the stairs and his hand rose to his heart. He sprang back up the steps. Fumblingly he pulled off his glove so that he might take her hand and kiss it. But the 'Princess' only looked at him with large, round eyes as blue as the summer sea and clasped her hands tightly behind her back. "Would . . . I mean, shall I . . . may I escort you to meet the King?" he said.

"Oh, couldn't we dance first?" whispered Cinderella, not realising that she was speaking to the Prince. "I'm terrified of meeting the King or the Prince, but you have such a kind, good face: I'm sure I should get up my courage if you would just dance one dance with me." The Prince, who had never been asked to dance before, laughed with delight, and escorted her to the dance floor where he swept her round in the dizzying whirl of music.

No wonder the time went fast. The one dance she had asked for turned into two and then into twenty and still the kind young man did not put her to the agony of meeting the King or the Prince. When she was thirsty, he brought her oranges. "The rarest fruit in my . . . in the kingdom," he explained. Cinderella took them and sat down beside her father and stepsisters, and split the golden skins and pulled apart the golden segments, sharing them equally.

Gouda and Gorgonzola were so busy gazing at the outlandish fruit in their hands, greedily crushing out the juice with curling tongues, that they did not even look the 'Princess' in the face. (Besides, loveliness only made them jealous.)

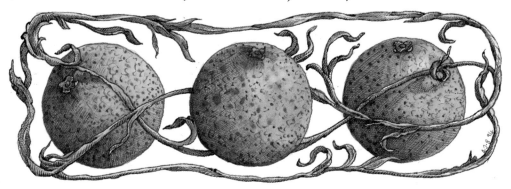

One by one the dancers drifted away to other rooms, to the banqueting table, to the balcony and gardens. They could see perfectly well that the Prince wanted to be alone with the beautiful stranger. Of course the ugly stepsisters were the last to go: they never noticed anything to do with other people.

"You're so beautiful," said the Prince at last.

"Oh, my dress you mean? Yes, isn't it the most wonderful dress you ever saw? My . . . someone gave it to me. Have you seen the shoes? I bet you never saw glass shoes before!"

"I never did," he admitted, laughing, then realising she still did not know who he was, he went on, "This is foolish. We've danced together all evening and I don't even know your name."

"I – " What could she say? "They call me – " How could she say 'Cinderella' – scullery maid? Little Miss Nobody who warmed her feet in the ashes?

"I'm sorry, I've kept you to myself all evening," he said (though he did not sound very apologetic), "but I had to be sure."

"Oh, it's been wonderful!" she cried, touching the buttons on his jacket one by one. "Sure of what?"

"Sure I had made the right choice. You know, I suppose, that I love you?"

"Oh no! You can't . . . !"

"Why? You're not in love with someone else, are you?"

"No! But you can't possibly love me . . . at least, not as much as I love you." The Prince's face broke into a smile. He had hardly dared to hope the evening would bring him such an exquisite Princess. "But there's something I really ought to tell you . . ."

DONG! DONG! went the great clock bell.

DONG! DONG!

Midnight!

"I must go! I have to go! I can't stay! I'm sorry! I'm sorry!" She broke away from the Prince, as though to stay another moment would cost her her life. She fled up the staircase. *DONG! DONG!* the clock kept on striking. Cinderella ran out into the night air and a shock of cold like icewater. *DONG! DONG!*

"Come back!" cried the Prince. "My dear, dearest whoever-you-are... I don't know who you are!" he gasped,

and tried to run after her. But Gouda and Gorgonzola, hoping to dazzle him with their own beauty, stepped in front of him and barred his way. *DONG! DONG!* He dodged this way and that, while they tittered and giggled and curtsied and fluttered their eyelids.

"Come back! I love you!" called the Prince. But Cinderella did not even look round. She ran on as if wolves were chasing her – so fast that she stumbled and fell down the palace steps of white marble. Rolling over and over she landed – bump – against the wheels of her coppery coach. She clambered inside and the six white horses sprang instantly into a gallop. *DONG! DONG!*

The reins went slack. The doors of the coach fell outwards and the wheels rolled away in four separate directions. The coach lizards fell on Cinderella's head, and there she sat on the muddy road, in a hand-me-down dress and one glass shoe.

One shoe? Why should her glass slipper have kept its magic after midnight? And where was the other one?

Cinderella took off the one remaining slipper and put it in her pocket before running home barefoot.

The Prince, too, ran out into the cold darkness, still calling, still begging his mysterious dance partner to come back to him. When he could see no trace of her, he put his head in his hands and turned back towards the lights and music.

But wait a minute! What was that, glittering on the steps like a fallen sliver of moon? A glass slipper – so tiny that it might have belonged to a child. "It's hers! She showed me! I must find her! I must!" And though his guests and his family and his courtiers tried to reason with him the Prince was adamant. "Whomsoever the shoe fits, I shall marry. Carry it through the land on a crimson cushion, to every house and home. If Fate decrees we shall marry, the shoe will find its owner, my heart will find its one desire, and I shall find my bride!"

What a stir that caused! The glass slipper carried from door to door, tried on by every lady in the land. And a royal crown for the girl whose foot fitted the tiny slipper. What a temptation! Women were quite ready to crush and crumple their feet into the little shoe, whatever pain it cost them. Gouda and Gorgonzola were quite sure they could do it, if only they soaked their feet in vinegar, put butter on their heels and rammed home their toes

hard and deep enough. The whole house was full of their shrieks and impatience as they awaited the arrival of the Prince's pageboy.

"*Cinderella! The DOOR!!!*" they screamed, peering out of the window at the boy bearing the crimson cushion. "This is our greatest hour! This is what we've always deserved! This is our shining day!"

"But you aren't the pretty girl the Prince danced with," said their father, bewildered. "We met her. She sat with us and gave us pieces of orange."

"What's *that* got to do with anything?" demanded Gorgonzola. "He'll never know the difference. Besides, he's said he'll marry 'whomsoever the shoe fits'. So that's his bad luck, isn't it? He shouldn't make such rash promises. Cinderella! Get out of sight, immediately. You make the place look untidy."

So Cinderella slipped out of sight. Her hand, too, slipped out of sight – into the apron pocket where she kept the other glass slipper, that treasured souvenir of her happiest night. She would not be allowed to try on the slipper, of course. But then what would the Prince think, anyway, if he knew that his dancing partner was nothing but a scullery maid? A prince! If only she had known. If only he were someone less grand, someone she might have lived in hope of meeting again.

Gouda grabbed the slipper off its cushion and crammed it on to her foot. But you could no more fit a cat into a mousehole.

Gorgonzola snatched it away from her. "Don't be ridiculous, woman. Who'd ever mistake *you* for a mysterious princess? You know it was me, all along. Didn't I sit beside you, feeding you pieces of orange?" She began to wriggle her foot into the glass slipper. But you could no more fit a horse into a kennel. She and Gouda came to blows, fighting over the shoe, while the page tried to snatch it back and continue his endless, fruitless search.

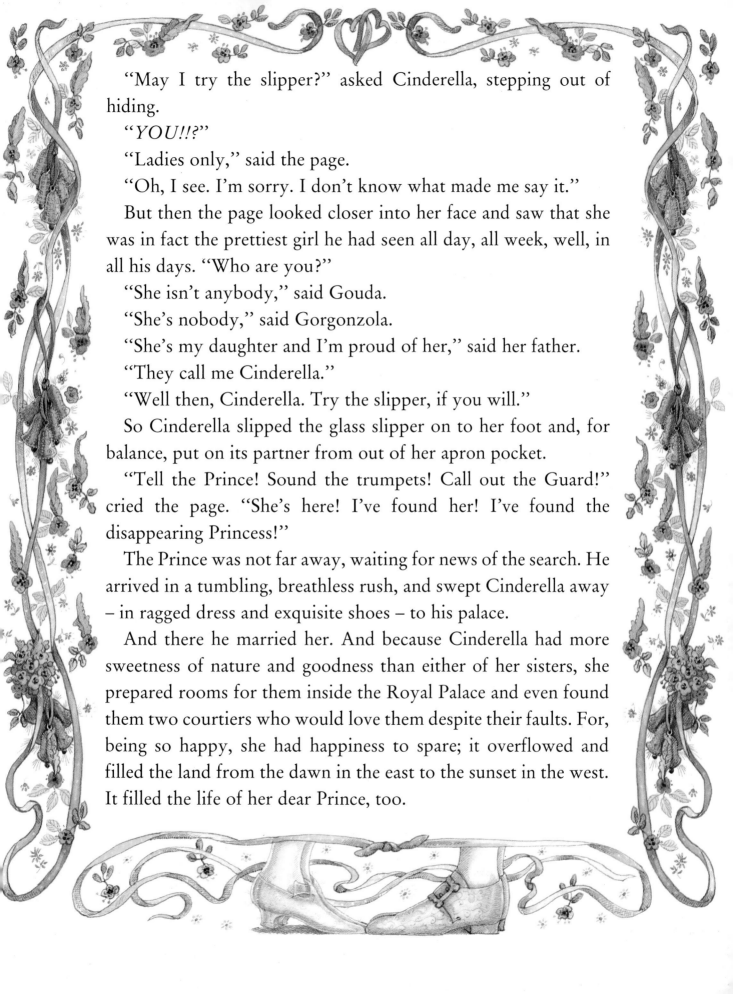

"May I try the slipper?" asked Cinderella, stepping out of hiding.

"*YOU!!?*"

"Ladies only," said the page.

"Oh, I see. I'm sorry. I don't know what made me say it."

But then the page looked closer into her face and saw that she was in fact the prettiest girl he had seen all day, all week, well, in all his days. "Who are you?"

"She isn't anybody," said Gouda.

"She's nobody," said Gorgonzola.

"She's my daughter and I'm proud of her," said her father.

"They call me Cinderella."

"Well then, Cinderella. Try the slipper, if you will."

So Cinderella slipped the glass slipper on to her foot and, for balance, put on its partner from out of her apron pocket.

"Tell the Prince! Sound the trumpets! Call out the Guard!" cried the page. "She's here! I've found her! I've found the disappearing Princess!"

The Prince was not far away, waiting for news of the search. He arrived in a tumbling, breathless rush, and swept Cinderella away – in ragged dress and exquisite shoes – to his palace.

And there he married her. And because Cinderella had more sweetness of nature and goodness than either of her sisters, she prepared rooms for them inside the Royal Palace and even found them two courtiers who would love them despite their faults. For, being so happy, she had happiness to spare; it overflowed and filled the land from the dawn in the east to the sunset in the west. It filled the life of her dear Prince, too.

LA SYLPHIDE

Amid the heather-purple folds of the Scottish highlands, shrouded in rainy mists, the houses are scattered about like sheep, but not so plentifully. Such a small world of friends and neighbours that it is hard for two grown people to meet who have never met before. Take James and Effie. They knew each other for years before they got engaged. Everyone always said they would marry. There seemed nothing against it. So they did. At least the wedding was fixed for June, and their friends and relations looked forward happily to the dancing, the party, the whisky and the food. James and Effie looked forward to it too, pretty much.

Only Gurn, their friend, was breaking his heart. For he had always loved Effie, with a dogged, unwavering devotion, and dearly wished he could be the groom and James the best man. He was simply not clever enough to put his feelings into pretty words.

So James was the lucky man. James was the one sitting beside his hearth that June morning, in his best highland kilt, lace jabot and silver-buttoned jacket, thinking about the happiness in store. At least he should have been thinking about it. But the flickering flames in the grate seemed to make pictures, dancing pictures. Then a ray of light bouncing off the mirror made a yellow puddle on the wall. He chased it with his eyes and found it looked uncommonly like a creature, a winged creature, a girl dressed all in white gossamer. He gazed and gazed, at her slender ankles, tiny waist, willowy movements and pale mysterious face. And as he stared, he made unkind, unavoidable comparisons with bonny, bouncing Effie of the red cheeks and starched pinafore.

Where did it come from that fairy form, dancing and prancing just out of the corner of his eye? Was it wishful thinking that made him picture her there, his ideal love, the kind of girl he had never met among the milk pails and pig runs of the glens? The kind he had always dreamed of meeting. The vision flitted into the hearth and away up the chimney like a snatch of pale smoke. "Too late for second thoughts, McKenzie," James told himself. "Effie will be here in a moment. Her wedding dress is lying on the bed upstairs, ready and waiting."

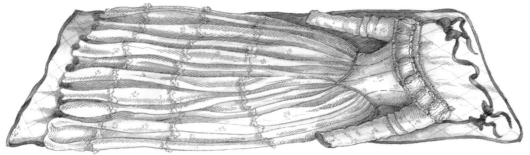

He closed his eyes and tried to picture the Sylph again. But then Effie arrived, and Gurn. And other friends soon followed, with wedding presents such as a fine tartan shawl for Effie. They were so overbrimming with good wishes that their kindness and laughter might well have swept James back into cheerful mood. If only Old Madge had stayed away.

Madge the Crone was a fortune-teller. She had a way of inviting herself along to weddings, christenings and harvest suppers, offering to tell fortunes to anyone who would cross her palm with silver. She was as warty and hunched as a toad, with rat's-tail hair and a nose like a rusty doorknocker. The smell that hung, fungusy, from her ragged clothes was of wet sheep and mildew and cooking cabbage. "Fortunes! Fortunes? Who wants their fortune told on this bright, lucky day?"

"You shall have a long and happy marriage, my dear," Madge told Effie, stroking her soft pink palm. Then, lifting one gnarled finger and pointing it at James, she cackled, *"But not to him!"* And before James could pick up the fireside broom and catch her a blow with it, Old Madge scurried out of the house cackling and cursing. Effie ran happily upstairs to put on her dress, her friends ran off to play their own part in the wedding preparations, and once again James found himself alone.

Alone? Why then should he feel a pair of eyes watching him from high overhead. Why did his heart beat faster?

Before he even looked around he knew what he would see in the high window of his living room: a Sylph dressed all in white, swooping towards him on wide white wings. The room was filled with a sweet, soundless music, and they danced to the beating of their hearts which kept perfect time with one another.

"I love you, James McKenzie. I have loved you many years now, since I first saw you amid the heather."

"And I love you, Sylph. That's what you are, isn't it? A spirit of the air? I think I've loved you since I was born. You've been there in every dream I've ever dreamed, waking or sleeping."

"Then don't marry Effie today. That's why I came here. That's why I had to show myself today! Don't marry her! I think I should die if you were to marry another woman!"

As if by way of an answer, James took her in his arms and kissed her, little realising that Gurn was standing in the doorway behind him.

It was not horror or disapproval that flooded Gurn's heart, but a sudden surge of hope. What if Effie were to see such a sight? How would she feel towards her handsome bridegroom then? Here was Gurn's great chance to win her away from James and marry her himself!

Silently he backed out of the doorway and leapt upstairs, snatched Effie, half dressed, by the hand and positively hauled her after him. "Come and see what manner of man you chose when you could have chosen me!"

Together they burst into the living room.

James stood on the hearthrug, his forehead damp with guilty sweat, his face flushed, his breathing quick and embarrassed.

"Where is she? Where've you hidden her?" demanded Gurn. "Where's that fancy woman of yours, eh?"

"I don't know what you're talking about. I – "

Hearing footsteps on the stairs, the Sylph had jumped into the fireside chair and James had hastily thrown Effie's new shawl over her to hide her. Wild-eyed with jealous triumph, Gurn searched about the room. When he saw the suspicious drape of the shawl over the chairback he gave a great crowing laugh. "Well and who have we *here*?" He could tell from James's face that he had guessed right, and he snatched the shawl away.

Nothing. No one. The Sylph had disappeared. James was every bit as surprised as Gurn, but he quickly hid it, telling Gurn it was a remarkably cruel joke to play on Effie. Effie herself was furious. Her hair only half fastened, her dress still unbuttoned, she told Gurn off in no uncertain terms for making such a fool and a nuisance of himself. Her friends, fetched back in by all the noise, were hard put to soothe her – until the piper struck up the music.

With whoops and leaps, they danced all the traditional dances their grandparents and neighbours had been dancing at weddings since ever weddings began.

And no one but James saw the white figure, dressed in filmy gauze, who joined in their dance, who darted beneath the arches of arms, skipping to and fro. She was the partner he wanted in life; *hers* was the beauty that held him spellbound. Fortunately Effie was too swallowed up by her own blind happiness to see that his eyes were not on her, that his feet were dancing to a different, fairy music.

The minister of religion arrived. The friends pressed close round bride and groom, like the hands round a bouquet. Forget the Sylph, James McKenzie. This is reality. Everything else is imaginary. Here is the minister. Here is your wedding day. Here is bonny Effie. Here is the ring. Forget the Sylph, James McKenzie, and put on the ring, or what excuse will you give? That you imagine yourself in love with a fairy?

Just as the ring was about to slip over Effie's finger, something or someone invisible snatched it away. The high window blew wide open with a slam, and a flickering reflection from the mirror – or was it smoke from the fire? – slipped through the narrow space into the wide mauve sky beyond.

Then James forgot his bride, his friends, his wedding, and rushed after the Sylph, his thoughts fixed only on following his dream. The wedding guests could make no sense of what was happening, until Gurn told them, delighting in their horror, "He's gone to find his lover, that's what!" It was malicious and spiteful. Effie fell swooning at his feet.

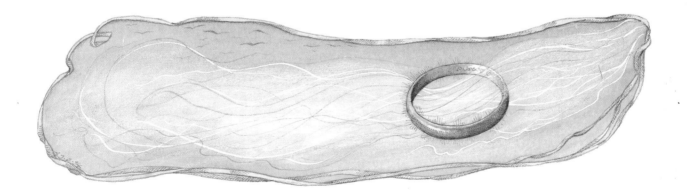

Through the woods ran James. Sometimes the Sylph was as far distant as a patch of cloud in the sky. Sometimes she was so close that her dress brushed his outstretched hands. Still, he could no more catch hold of it than cold, running water.

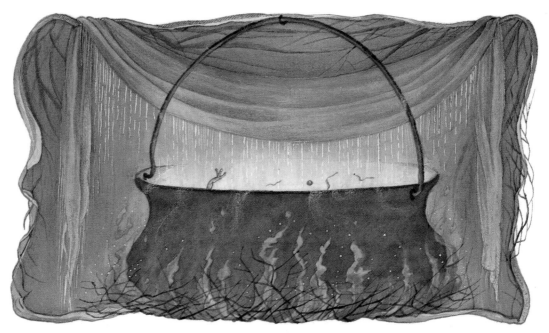

In his headlong dash, he made a gruesome discovery: the lair of Old Madge the hag – and not just hers, either, but the gathering place of all the local witches.

You see, Madge was no harmless old crone. She was one of a sisterhood of witches. Theirs was the hot wickedness bubbling in that great iron cauldron. Theirs was the shawl of iridescent rainbow dyes, just now drawn from the cauldron and dangling and dazzling from the tongs in Madge's hands. "What's wrong, James McKenzie? Can't you catch your fairy lover? Come here and I'll help you. You need my help now, don't you? Knew you would."

"Can you help me?" he panted. "Can you really? I came after her and yet she keeps running away! Why won't she come to me? Why won't she wait for me?"

"Maybe you haven't given her a token of your love," said the old crone in her creaking voice. "Don't you know how women like presents? Now take this shawl . . . With it you could dock her wings as easily as you dock the tails off your woolly sheep."

"I wouldn't like to hurt her – not give her any pain!"

"Oh, don't fret about that. 'Twill wrap her round soft as baby swaddling, you take my word, young man. You just see if she don't come for a thing this pretty, and stay for ever once she's come?" The laugh she laughed turned James's blood to ice. But he was so eager to please his Sylph that he took the shawl and stood whirling it over his head, a great flag of colour writing against the sky: "I LOVE YOU, SYLPHIDE! COME TO ME!"

The colours mesmerised her. She could not resist. She came.

"Why did you run from me? Has your love changed towards me?" he called out to her.

The Sylph crept closer, sat down at his feet. "Oh, James, it's hard for me. If I marry a mortal, I must leave behind my airy playmates. It's a great deal to give up . . . I had to make sure you cared enough for me to risk the danger of the forest and chase me no matter where. I see you do love me, just as I love you. What's that you're holding?"

"A present for you," said James. "A token of my love." And he folded the shawl lovingly round her shoulders, over her white, gauzy wings.

"It's beautiful . . . so pretty . . . so warm . . . so . . . Aghh!" The Sylph cast him a look full of terror and puzzlement. "Why? Why have you done this?" she cried. She tried to throw off the shawl, but it cleaved to her like a twist of fire. Her white wings scorched and dropped to the ground. She arched her back, writhed in

agony, the shawl's evil magic poisoning her willowy body. Then, crying out his name once more, she fell dead at his feet.

Like a storm of butterflies, the whole tribe of sylphs swarmed into the clearing, a dazzling choir of white, too painfully bright. They looked at James with eyes full of unforgiving reproach, then carried their sister away, shoulder high.

James knelt among the rotting leaves, his shoulders bent in misery, his fists beating the ground. But not everyone shared his sorrow. Old Madge and the witches danced with delight.

And through the glen wove a band of happy friends. It was Effie's wedding day, after all, even though she had decided at the last moment to marry the faithful Gurn instead of the faithless, dreaming James McKenzie.

THE NUTCRACKER

Once upon a time there was a perfect Christmas. Oh, it did not start very well, but for Clara Stahlbaum it was to be the Christmas she would remember for the rest of her life, and describe to her own children as if it were a fairy tale – which indeed it was, in a way.

Christmas was always magical in the Stahlbaum house. Clara and Fritz looked forward to it for weeks beforehand, talked of nothing else. On Christmas Eve they peeped down through the banisters to see ladies arriving in velvet dresses and fur muffs, men carrying tall hats dusty with snow – and lots of children too excited to behave nicely. Clara and Fritz ran downstairs to greet their friends and to be ready, there – right there on the threshhold – when the doors of the dining room were opened.

All day the doors had been locked, sealing in the secrets of Christmas. With a flood of light that spilled out into the hall, they swung open now. Why, it hardly looked like the dining room at all, but some magical garden, the tree spangled with candles, the wineglasses glittering like ice on the snow-white tablecloth, the flowers filling every alcove, mantelpiece and sill. Piled around the base of the tree was a mountain of presents in bright wrappings. And there, at the top of the tree, her wand outstretched as if she had just decorated the room by magic, balanced the Christmas Fairy, her head made of a sugar plum and her dress out of spun sugar.

For Clara there was a dress and a cot for her dolls, a sugar cane – and the one gift she had wanted more than anything in the world: a pair of pink ballet shoes so beautiful they made her eyes gleam with tears. Naturally, Clara started the dancing.

Suddenly, just as the clock in the hall struck nine, all the candles guttered in a fierce, cold draught that made everybody shudder. For a moment the room was almost dark. Something black brushed past Mama Stahlbaum and she gave a little shriek. Then the candles flared up again and there stood a tall, thin old man all in black, his face hidden by a huge snow-sodden hood, a black sack at his feet. There was a dreadful silence.

"Drossy!" cried Clara. "It's Uncle Drosselmeyer!" And she ran and hugged the old man. "I wasn't frightened one bit!"

"Drosselmeyer, you old rogue!" bellowed Papa Stahlbaum. "How you do like to cause a stir!" But everyone was delighted to see the old Professor. No Christmas was quite complete without him – or his famous presents.

No toyshop in the world ever sold toys as splendid as the toys the Professor made. This Christmas Eve, however, Professor Drosselmeyer had brought more than presents to the party.

"Let me introduce you to my nephew, Karl."

"Never mind him," said Fritz. "What have you brought me?"

"I'm very pleased to meet you, Karl," said Clara, and curtsied to the young man. What a handsome boy! What a gentle smile. Why can't Fritz be more like him? Clara found herself thinking.

"Well then, let's see . . ." Uncle Drossy sank his beaky nose into the deep, black sack. "For my godchildren I have this year a clockwork mouse . . ."

"I'll have that!" cried Fritz and snatched it.

"A hobby horse to *share*," said Drosselmeyer sternly.

"Oh, *I'll* have that!" cried Fritz and, throwing the mouse aside, snatched up the hobby horse.

"A box of toy soldiers . . ."

The hobby horse was flung down and Fritz scattered all the soldiers about – beautiful models painted with scarlet uniforms, cockaded hats, glossy boots and bandoleers with buckles of gold.

"But this is just for my little Clara," said Drossy. "Miss Clara – meet Captain Kracko!" He laid the toy in her arms: another soldier, but much bigger than the others and carved of wood. His head was enormous, with a gigantic set of white teeth fixed in a big grin. The back flaps of his jacket lifted up, and as they did so Captain Kracko's mouth dropped open. "Well? He's hungry. Won't you offer the poor gentleman a nut to eat?" suggested Drossy. Clara popped in a little hazelnut and, with a snap of his coat-tails, and a smack of his lips, Captain Kracko shelled the nut.

"A nutcracker! Just what I need!" shouted Fritz, tearing across the room.

"No, no! This is Clara's special toy," said Uncle Drossy firmly.

"*Hers?* A soldier for a girl?" Fritz was so put out that he snatched the nutcracker anyway and forced a huge walnut between its jaws. Then, when he could not make the crackers close, he smashed its gaping head against the floor.

Clara burst into such tears that Christmas itself might have lain there on the floor, broken past repair.

Karl Drosselmeyer did what he could. He bandaged the wounded soldier with a giant pocket handkerchief, and Clara laid him in her new doll's crib. Uncle Drossy called for dancing, and the little tragedy seemed forgotten as the waltzes began.

But Clara did not forget, could not forget. Even after the guests had said goodnight, the candles had gone out, the family had climbed to their beds, and the big house had fallen quiet, Clara could not put the wounded Captain out of her mind. She had to creep downstairs and see if his poor head was truly broken past mending.

It was midnight. Uncle Drossy's eerie clock was just striking the hour as she entered the dining room. The great tree loomed darkly in front of the window. A smouldering log rolled in the grate. Clara tucked up Captain Kracko in his little bed and kissed his big, lopsided mouth. "Poor dear," she yawned, exhausted. "I love you anyway, broken or not." The tree rustled its branches.

And then another noise! A sudden movement by the skirting board. A scuttering of claws. Clara leapt on to the great sofa and drew her nightdress tight round her feet. A mouse!

Scared of a little mouse? You would have been, too, if you had seen it. For it was *huge* – bigger than a rat, bigger than a cat, bigger than a dog – bigger, when it had finished growing, than Clara herself. In one crooked claw it held a sabre, and between its tattered ears balanced a golden crown. "Advance, mice, and kill the enemy while he's sleeping!" rasped the Mouse King.

"Sleeping? That's what you think!" cried a fearless voice, and Captain Kracko leapt to his feet.

Was it him? Could it be? He seemed so much taller, almost of a height with the Mouse King. And the toy soldiers who sprang to arms at his rallying cry were at least as tall as Clara.

The mice charged. The troopers fixed silver bayonets to their rifles and launched a counterstrike. Blood-curdling war cries from the Mouse King mingled with stirring shouts from the Captain. Clara curled down among the cushions at first, but the fight became so thrilling that she knelt up and beat with her fists on the

sofaback: "Come on, soldiers! You can trounce them! *Oh no!*"

An unlucky slip sent the Captain sprawling, and the Mouse King was on him in an instant with slashing sabre cuts that knocked the Captain's sword from his hand. There was no time to lose. Clara pulled off her slipper and threw it – whack! – at the back of that mousey head.

The whiskers twitched. The clawed feet staggered this way and that. The golden crown went rolling. Captain Kracko jumped to his feet and his troopers rallied round him. They drove the mice off in one last fearsome attack, which sent the cowards squealing and squeaking back to their underground kingdom to lick their wounds.

"You have saved the day, lady!" cried the Captain, still breathless as he saluted her and bowed smartly. With a click of his heels he said, "Permit me to crown you with the captured crown of the Mouse King, and to escort you to the Queen, that she may thank you in person for your bravery!"

"The *Queen*?" gasped Clara.

"Naturally. My mother, the Queen of my country. Across the Lemonade Ocean. In the Land of Sweets."

She stared at the Captain and, all at once, realised that he was not simply a pair of nutcrackers, not even just a handsome soldier, but a prince. Oddly he bore a strong likeness to old Drosselmeyer's nephew Karl. The two could almost have been brothers.

Off they set, in a huge hollow walnut shell with sails of green angelica and a crew of scarlet-coated soldiers. The Lemonade Ocean fizzed beneath the prow, and a wake of silver bubbles stretched out behind.

All trace of Clara's house was hidden by a sudden swirl of snowflakes.

Festivities were already in hand in the Kingdom of Sweets, to celebrate the great victory over the mice. Bunting hung in the streets and crowds waving flags lined the waterfront as the walnut-shell boat came into harbour. As Clara stepped ashore, a little gingerbread boy presented her with a bouquet of icing-sugar flowers and hundreds of thousands of hundreds-and-thousands showered down from the open windows of every house. On a green marzipan lawn, under a meringue canopy, a delicious banquet of sweets had been laid along a white-clothed table. Many coffers of the state treasury had been emptied of their golden chocolate coins to pay for the celebrations.

Someone very special was waiting to lead Clara and the Prince before the Queen: it was the Sugar Plum Fairy – tall, beautiful, willowy, and dressed in a gown more glistening than liquid sugar. "Now don't be shy," she told Clara, "but do speak up."

Clara curtsied low to the Queen – a magnificent, jolly lady whose dress and hair were bejewelled with sweets of every colour.

"Mother, may I present Miss Clara Stahlbaum, whose bravery and quick thinking saved the day!" declared Prince Kracko.

"Welcome, welcome!" cried the Queen, jumping up out of her chair and bustling down the red carpet. "I hear I have you to thank for the safe return of my dear Kracko. Thank you, thank you. A million times, thank you." She wrapped Clara in the warmest of hugs and laid a large, loud kiss on her forehead.

With a clap of her hands, the Sugar Plum Fairy summoned hot chocolate, coffee and tea for the guests of honour. But the moment the drinks were set down on the table, they began to dance! Spanish chocolate, Arabian coffee and China tea all danced in their own distinctive way, the cups spinning on their saucers – but never a drop spilt.

Then the sugar canes came, in candystripe suits of the sort gentlemen wear on the sea front to walk arm in arm with their ladies.

Mrs Bonbon (who always keeps her children under her black-and-white crinoline) let them all loose to dance, and Clara laughed and clapped to see how they did their party-pieces then dived back to the safety of their mother's skirts. The flowers came out to waltz, too, on the greensward – not the sort of flowers you see

in gardens, but the kind that curl their sugar petals on the snowy icing of Christmas cakes. Some snow fell that afternoon, but it was only a dusting of icing sugar for, in the Land of Sweets, it was able to be both Christmas and summer at the same time.

The prettiest dance of all was the one the Sugar Plum Fairy danced with her own dashing cavalier. Clara stared and stared, until Prince Kracko leaned across and whispered, "They are in love, you know." After that, she did not like to stare so very hard, in case she offended them.

"What perfectly beautiful ballet shoes!" exclaimed the Queen all of a sudden, looking at Clara's feet. "Won't you dance for us too?"

"Oh, *I* can't dance, not properly! Not yet, at least. These were a Christmas present from my Uncle Drosselmeyer."

"Oh yes, the dear man. We don't give each other presents at Christmas here, you know." Clara was hardly surprised. The people of the Land of Sweets seemed to have everything they could possibly want. "No, instead," the Queen went on, "the fairies grant us each a Christmas wish. A wish for each person in the Land of Sweets."

That gave Prince Kracko an idea. "Christmas is almost here! And Clara is in the Land of Sweets. She ought to be granted a wish!"

Clara blushed as red as the summer strawberries in her bowl, but the Sugar Plum Fairy answered his summons and waved her silvery wand over Clara's head. "And what is your Christmas wish, my dear?"

Clara did not hesitate for a moment. "Oh, I wish I could dance just as beautifully as you!" she cried. Prince Kracko rose from his chair and bowed low. He offered her his arm. "Oh, is it time to go already?" she asked in great disappointment.

The Prince laughed. "No, but I thought if you were going to dance you might need a partner."

So Prince Kracko and Clara danced – and a more beautiful dance you never saw. For Clara's wish was granted, and she found she was able to dance, in her new shoes, like the best of fairies, like the greatest of ballerinas. While they danced, Kracko looked at her in such a strange way, with his dark, chocolate-coloured eyes, that she felt a little shy and awkward. "What will *your* Christmas wish be, Prince Kracko?" Clara asked, longing to know.

"Oh, simply that I should dance with you again one day, here, in the Land of Sweets, when you are a grown woman."

They danced and danced. It was the Sugar Plum Fairy who had to remind them, "If Clara doesn't want to miss Christmas at her own house, she had better be going!"

So, sadly, Clara said goodbye to the Queen, and together she and the Prince made the return voyage in their walnut-shell boat. *Swish-swirl* went the foaming Lemonade Sea, a noise like the moving of pine trees in a winter forest. The snow in the air was so brightly moonlit that she had to close her eyes, and the movement of the boat rocked her, rocked her, rocked her like her new toy Christmas cradle.

When Clara opened her eyes again, her cheek was pressed not to the velvet of the Prince's scarlet jacket but to the plush cushion of the sofa. The damaged nutcrackers lay tucked under her arm, while the house still slept in the grey light of a snowy Christmas dawn.

You think she had just been dreaming, don't you?

Then how did Captain Kracko's jaw come to be mended? Good as new. And why was there a sticky red kiss right in the middle of her forehead?

ROMEO AND JULIET

They say that Love lives next door to Hate. It certainly seemed to, those hot days long ago in Verona. The Italian sun overhead kindled love and squabbles in equal quantities. Either the young men were head over heels in love or they were brawling with one another in the streets. Either they were swearing eternal love or vowing revenge for some little offence.

The quarrelling had gone on so long between the Capulet family and the Montagues that no one could even remember what had begun it. But every so often the young men of each family, always eager to show off, would pick a fight. A nose was broken, a head cut, a tunic torn. And with every fight the hatred between the families grew. Such a waste, when there are so much better things to do with a sunny day.

"Oh, how I adore her!" cried Romeo. His friend Mercutio groaned and gave him a push. Romeo was always in love with someone right up to his nose. Today it was Rosaline. Tomorrow it would be someone else.

All of a sudden, like a hot gust of wind, a gang of boys swaggered into the marketplace. It was that darling-boy of the Capulets, Tybalt, with his serving men, Peter, Samson and Gregory. They were spoiling for a fight. Insults flew – rude names, gestures, challenges: "You wouldn't dare, you smear of lard!"

"Who wouldn't? Think I couldn't finish you?"

"When? You never draw that sword of yours! Don't know why you wear it if you don't dare use it. To fwighten off the nasty bullies, is it? Ah, diddums." Sensible parents would have put a swift stop to it. But the Lords Montague and Capulet were just as deeply bogged down in the foolish family feud as their sons. In the end, swords were drawn.

"*Stop!*"

Every knee in the marketplace bent in a respectful bow. It was the Prince of Verona. "Montagues! Capulets! You ought to be ashamed of yourselves! How many years do you mean to carry on this little war of yours within my city precincts? I've had enough of it! Finish it here and now! Shake hands and call a peace before one of you does something we all regret."

The Capulets drew back. The Montagues went on their way. But the hatred simmered in the streets like a bad smell on a hot day.

Meanwhile another member of the Capulet family sat dreaming, without a thought in the world for quarrels or fights. Oh, Juliet knew about the feud. She even supposed she hated the Montagues, because the rest of her family hated them. But she had far more important things on her mind. Young as she was – just fourteen – her parents considered her old enough to marry. Marry! Her dear old nurse knew a thing or two about marriage. But what she said sounded wonderfully strange to Juliet, who had hardly even talked to a boy other than her cousin Tybalt. They laughed a lot, old Nursey and little Juliet. It was rather sad to see how much closer Juliet felt to the old serving woman than to her own mother and father.

Grand and elegant, awesome . . . and just a little cold, Lord and Lady Capulet swept into Juliet's room, bringing with them a visitor, a handsome young nobleman. "This is the Count Paris, my dear," said Lady Capulet to her daughter. "He has done us the very great honour of asking to meet you. Imagine! A Count wishing to know our little Juliet! You are a very lucky girl."

"Count Paris pays me a very great compliment," said Juliet politely, shivering with excitement. Oh yes, Juliet had much more important things on her mind than quarrels and family feuds.

The Count's visit to Verona called for a grand party – a ball at the Capulet house, with a hundred guests. The Montagues were not invited, of course. But Rosaline was.

"Rosaline! The love of my life! My joy! This is my chance to dance with her!" declared Romeo putting on a party mask.

"What, go to the ball at the Capulets' house? Isn't that a bit like climbing into the lion's mouth?" said Mercutio doubtfully.

"Yes, but what a laugh!" cried Benvolio. "To eat their Capulet food and jig to their Capulet music!"

"And to dance with Rosaline!" murmured Romeo, and both his friends groaned and put their fingers in their ears.

By the time the Montague gang got there, disguised in their masks, the dance was well under way. Juliet had danced with the Count Paris and everyone had heard the rumour of a marriage.

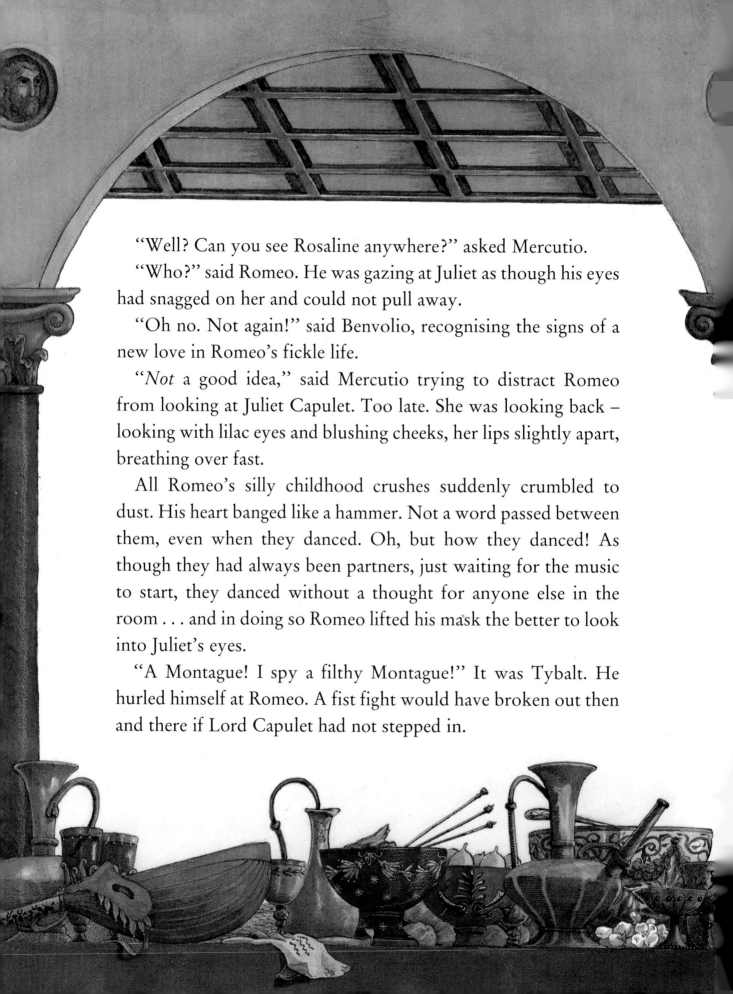

"Well? Can you see Rosaline anywhere?" asked Mercutio.

"Who?" said Romeo. He was gazing at Juliet as though his eyes had snagged on her and could not pull away.

"Oh no. Not again!" said Benvolio, recognising the signs of a new love in Romeo's fickle life.

"*Not* a good idea," said Mercutio trying to distract Romeo from looking at Juliet Capulet. Too late. She was looking back – looking with lilac eyes and blushing cheeks, her lips slightly apart, breathing over fast.

All Romeo's silly childhood crushes suddenly crumbled to dust. His heart banged like a hammer. Not a word passed between them, even when they danced. Oh, but how they danced! As though they had always been partners, just waiting for the music to start, they danced without a thought for anyone else in the room . . . and in doing so Romeo lifted his mask the better to look into Juliet's eyes.

"A Montague! I spy a filthy Montague!" It was Tybalt. He hurled himself at Romeo. A fist fight would have broken out then and there if Lord Capulet had not stepped in.

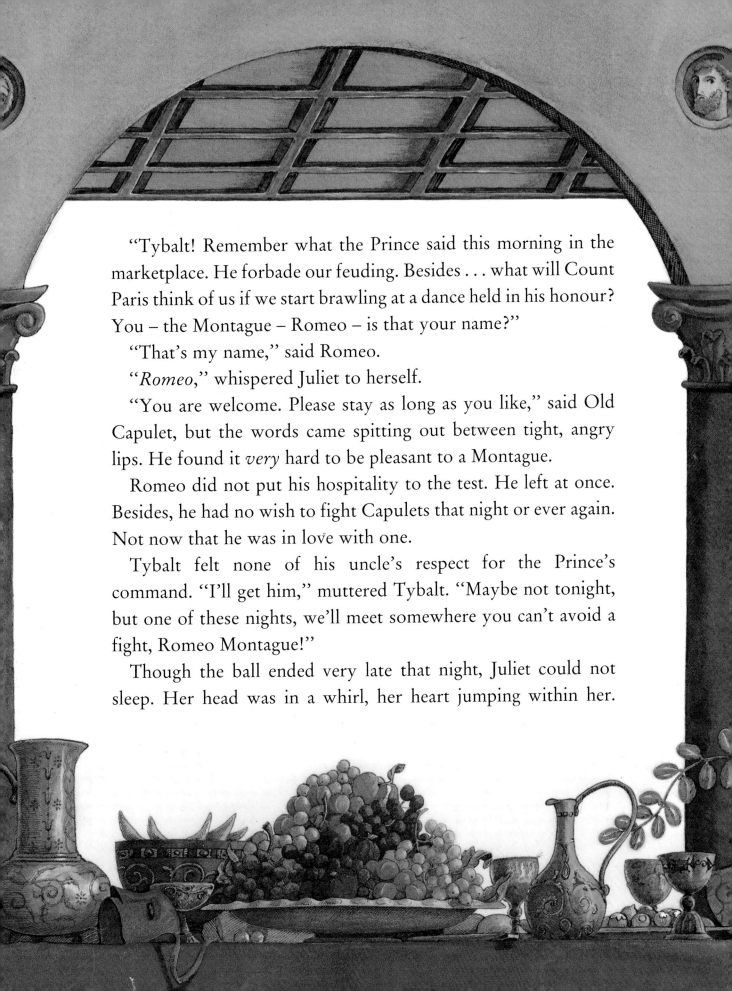

"Tybalt! Remember what the Prince said this morning in the marketplace. He forbade our feuding. Besides . . . what will Count Paris think of us if we start brawling at a dance held in his honour? You – the Montague – Romeo – is that your name?"

"That's my name," said Romeo.

"*Romeo*," whispered Juliet to herself.

"You are welcome. Please stay as long as you like," said Old Capulet, but the words came spitting out between tight, angry lips. He found it *very* hard to be pleasant to a Montague.

Romeo did not put his hospitality to the test. He left at once. Besides, he had no wish to fight Capulets that night or ever again. Not now that he was in love with one.

Tybalt felt none of his uncle's respect for the Prince's command. "I'll get him," muttered Tybalt. "Maybe not tonight, but one of these nights, we'll meet somewhere you can't avoid a fight, Romeo Montague!"

Though the ball ended very late that night, Juliet could not sleep. Her head was in a whirl, her heart jumping within her.

"Romeo," she said, tasting the name in her mouth. "Romeo. Romeo. Romeo." She stood on the balcony outside her bedroom windows and gazed over the moonlit orchards. "Romeo . . . Oh, why did you have to be a Montague? Why?"

"What does a name matter?" came a voice in reply. "What do families matter?" It was Romeo. He had hidden himself in the orchard, unable to tear himself away from the house containing his beloved Juliet. "Romeo and Juliet. Those are the only names that matter."

And he climbed up through the boughs of a blossomy tree to reach the balcony and taste Juliet's kisses, sweet as strawberries, against his mouth.

After that, no future seemed possible unless they could spend it together, for ever. Romeo and his Juliet, Juliet with her Romeo. He had never thought of actually *marrying* a girl before. Yet now he could think of nothing but marrying his Juliet. Would she have him? He tortured himself with doubts. He cursed himself for doubting her. The whole world seemed to be full of brides and grooms as he stumbled like a madman next day through the marketplace. A wedding party was in progress. He envied the happy couple; then again, he did not envy them at all, because he knew that no one in the history of the world had ever loved as deeply as Romeo and his Juliet.

Then through the crowds came old Nursey, that dear friend of Juliet's: the one person she could trust with the secret of her love. Nursey brought him a letter.

You have my love, you know that.
If you would like my hand in marriage,
I will marry you and be happy ever after.

"She wants to marry me!" shouted Romeo, kissing the letter.

"Shush! Speak softer, young gentleman," warned the old nurse. "A Capulet marry a Montague? There's a few people in Verona would want to put a stop to that. Me? I say True Love should have its way. So come with me – quickly – to the old Friar. Your Juliet's waiting there. To be your bride, if you'll have her . . . And if you won't, you're a downright fool, that's what I say, so there!" she added in a ferocious squawk. "Now keep your voice down, will you?"

So Romeo and Juliet were married, in a dark little room with no one near by but an old woman and the old monk who declared them man and wife. After blessing them, the Friar said, "I pray this love of yours will put a stop to the hate between your two families . . . Even so, you had best keep it secret until the time seems right for breaking the news. Otherwise you could be in serious trouble."

So both bride and groom kept secret their wedding, and parted company, agreeing to meet again that night on Juliet's balcony. Romeo met up with his friends – and was so happy they hardly recognised him.

"I'll wipe that grin off your face!" jibed a voice, surly and dangerous. It was Tybalt. He was wearing a sword and was determined to make Romeo pay for going to the party uninvited.

Romeo was horrified. Tybalt might not know it, but he was Romeo's own kin now – Juliet's cousin and therefore a cousin of his. "I don't want to fight you, Tybalt. I can't explain, but . . ."

"Oh, I can explain it!" jeered Tybalt. "You're a coward, that's what!"

"No, but I'd rather not fight you. I have my reasons."

Mercutio and Benvolio stared at him. Back down from a fight? It made them all look like cowards.

"I'll fight you if Romeo won't!" declared Mercutio and drew his sword.

"No, no, don't! Please!" said Romeo and held his friend's sword arm – just as Tybalt lunged. The sword's point sank deep into Mercutio's side. He died in Romeo's arms, cursing the two families whose feud had cut short his life.

Suddenly Romeo forgot any thought of kinship with Tybalt: he only knew that his best friend had been killed on his behalf. He snatched up a sword and, blind with rage, attacked Tybalt, running him clean through with the long, sharp blade.

The awful realisation of what he had done had hardly sunk in when the Prince of Verona himself arrived with a corps of soldiers. "I warned you Montagues to stop your feuding. Now look! My streets are stained with blood and the peace of my city has been shattered. Leave Verona by dawn tomorrow, boy, and never return. Never show your face here again – on pain of death!"

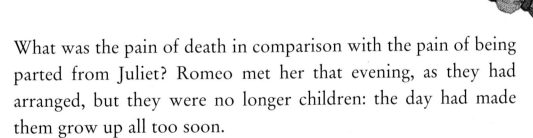

What was the pain of death in comparison with the pain of being parted from Juliet? Romeo met her that evening, as they had arranged, but they were no longer children: the day had made them grow up all too soon.

"How could you do it, you murderer!" she raged at him. "Kill Tybalt? Kill my own dear cousin? I've always loved Tybalt, ever since I remember. He was like a brother to me. How could you do it – you of all people? I hate you!" cried Juliet. Then she pulled him against her, her face pressed to his chest. "No! I'm sorry! I didn't say that! Don't listen to me! I could never hate you. I love you. You're my husband. You're my whole life. Exile! Take me with you. I can't lose you – not now! I'd sooner be dead, like Tybalt."

"No, no. We'll be together," said Romeo. "We will. I promise. I'll think of something. Soon, Juliet, soon. But it'll take time. I'll have to find work, somewhere to live. Then I'll send for you and we'll be together again. At least we have tonight."

So Romeo spent that night in Juliet's bedroom. But as dawn broke he had to leave.

No sooner had he slipped over the balcony rail than the bedroom door opened and Juliet's parents came in, along with the Count Paris. "Well, dear daughter. It is all agreed. The wedding is fixed for tomorrow. The Count here wishes to make you his wife and Countess."

"I do indeed!" said the Count, kissing her hand.

"Marry? No! No, I can't possibly! I mean . . . I *can't*!"

"Juliet!" snapped her father. "What is this nonsense?"

"She's just shy," said her mother soothingly. "All brides are nervous on the eve of their wedding. She's upset about her cousin Tybalt's death too, Count. That's what it is."

"No, it's not!" exclaimed Juliet, confused and flustered. How could she tell them she was married to a banished Montague who had just killed their favourite nephew? "I just can't. I mean, I won't. I mean – "

"Silence, child!" commanded Lord Capulet pompously. "You shame my house, talking like that. Either mend your behaviour or

I shall put you out of doors. I shall have nothing more to do with you! Come, Mother. Let us leave this foolish and ungrateful child to think over her disobedience and be sorry for it!"

Fourteen, and her parents threatening to disown her? Poor little Juliet was terrified. She ran to Friar Laurence and begged him to help.

Now Friar Laurence was not only a monk but a clever apothecary, too. He knew how to make all kinds of potions and cures. "I can think of a way to solve your problem," he said, "but you would have to be a very brave girl."

"Oh, I'd dare anything, *anything*, to be with Romeo again!"

"Very well. Here's a potion. Anyone who drinks it falls into a sleep so deep that they look quite dead. Drink this tonight. Tomorrow your family will think you have died in your sleep. They'll bury you in the family vault . . ."

"*Bury me? In my grave?*"

". . . and that's where I'll send Romeo to find you – and take you away with him to a new life." He sat down and pulled pen and paper in front of him. "I'll write to him now and explain everything. It would never do for him to think you were really dead! Ha ha ha!"

Juliet returned from her visit a changed girl. She went to her parents and said she was sorry for upsetting them. She said she was ready to marry the Count Paris whenever he chose.

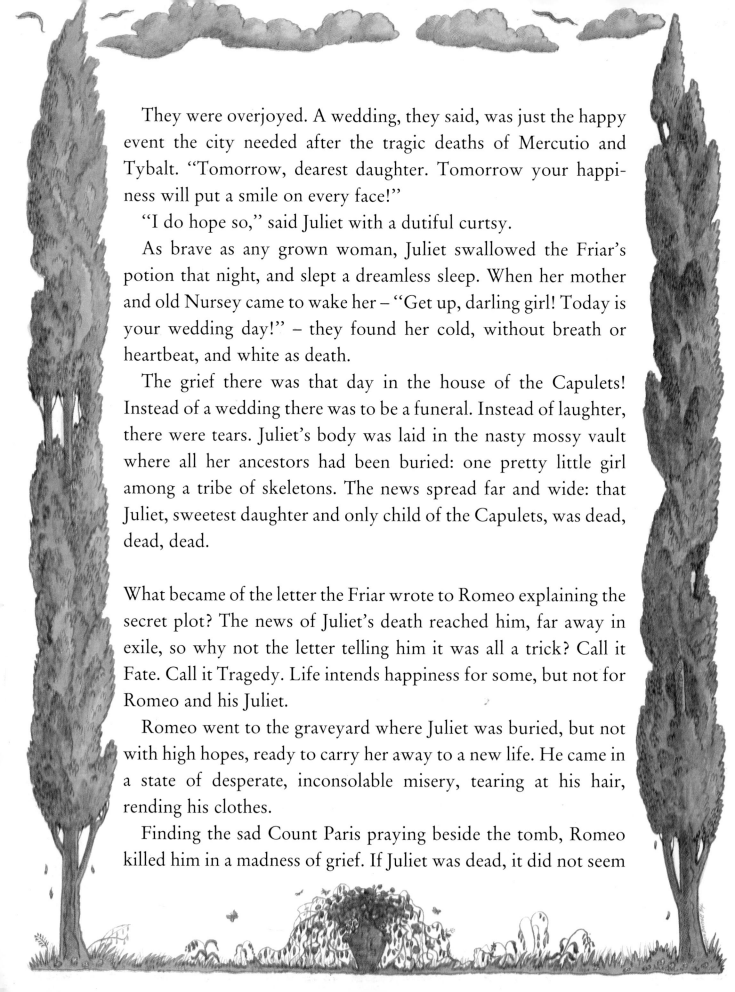

They were overjoyed. A wedding, they said, was just the happy event the city needed after the tragic deaths of Mercutio and Tybalt. "Tomorrow, dearest daughter. Tomorrow your happiness will put a smile on every face!"

"I do hope so," said Juliet with a dutiful curtsy.

As brave as any grown woman, Juliet swallowed the Friar's potion that night, and slept a dreamless sleep. When her mother and old Nursey came to wake her – "Get up, darling girl! Today is your wedding day!" – they found her cold, without breath or heartbeat, and white as death.

The grief there was that day in the house of the Capulets! Instead of a wedding there was to be a funeral. Instead of laughter, there were tears. Juliet's body was laid in the nasty mossy vault where all her ancestors had been buried: one pretty little girl among a tribe of skeletons. The news spread far and wide: that Juliet, sweetest daughter and only child of the Capulets, was dead, dead, dead.

What became of the letter the Friar wrote to Romeo explaining the secret plot? The news of Juliet's death reached him, far away in exile, so why not the letter telling him it was all a trick? Call it Fate. Call it Tragedy. Life intends happiness for some, but not for Romeo and his Juliet.

Romeo went to the graveyard where Juliet was buried, but not with high hopes, ready to carry her away to a new life. He came in a state of desperate, inconsolable misery, tearing at his hair, rending his clothes.

Finding the sad Count Paris praying beside the tomb, Romeo killed him in a madness of grief. If Juliet was dead, it did not seem right for anyone else to be left alive. *That* was why he had bought the poison on his journey. *That* was why, once he had seen his Juliet's body one last time, he drank the poison down without a moment's hesitation.

So when the effects of the Friar's clever potion wore off and Juliet woke up, she found Romeo beside her, just as she had expected. "Romeo? Wake up. You fell asleep waiting for the potion to wear off. Wake up, my dearest . . ." But when she touched him, she found all her bravery had been for nothing. "So cold? Your skin's like ice, my love." When she could not lift Romeo into her embrace, she laid her head on his chest instead, and drew his arms around her, chafing his cold, cold hands between her own.

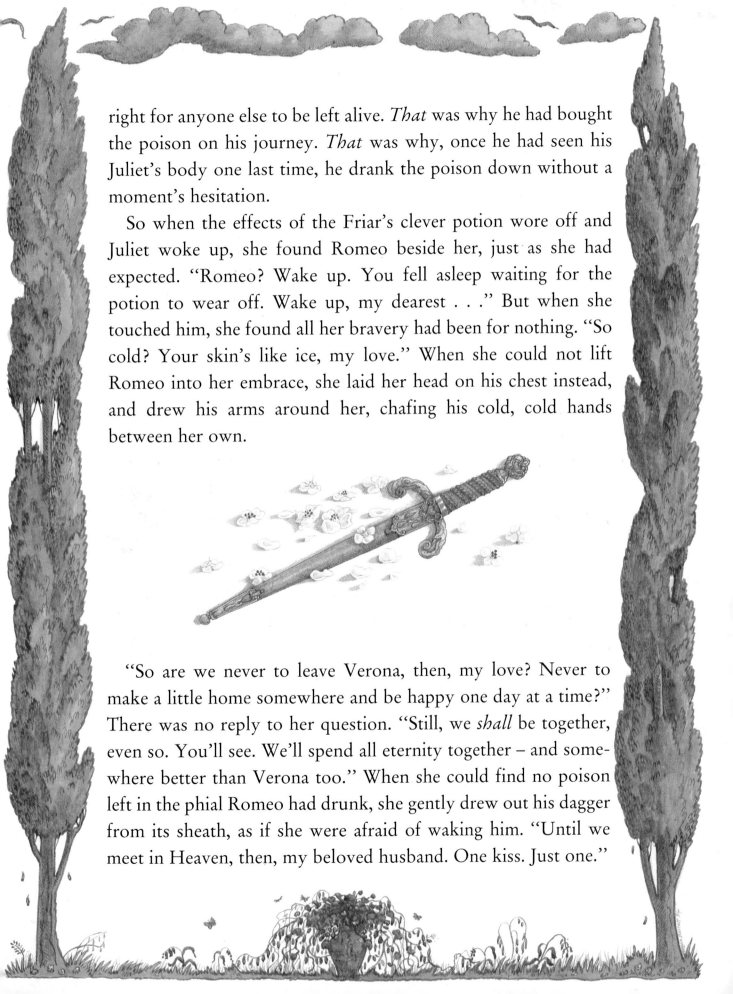

"So are we never to leave Verona, then, my love? Never to make a little home somewhere and be happy one day at a time?" There was no reply to her question. "Still, we *shall* be together, even so. You'll see. We'll spend all eternity together – and somewhere better than Verona too." When she could find no poison left in the phial Romeo had drunk, she gently drew out his dagger from its sheath, as if she were afraid of waking him. "Until we meet in Heaven, then, my beloved husband. One kiss. Just one."

It took Juliet hardly any courage at all to plunge the dagger into her own breast. "There," she whispered, "Now we two shall be left in peace."

Friar Laurence blamed himself, because of the letter going astray. But at least he had been right in hoping Romeo and Juliet's love would end the feud between their families. When the Capulets and the Montagues found out what had happened – how their children had died trying to overcome that stupid barrier of hatred – all the bitter rivalry crumbled away. They had too much in common to go on hating each other. Both families had lost their dearest children. Both families had stood in the way of True Love and been swept away by it like castles demolished by a flood.

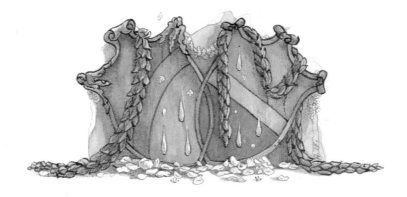

THE FIREBIRD

Once, beside the wall of an ancient castle, the sun shone down on a clearing amid dense, tall trees. You would have thought it was a garden left to run wild, for here and there stone statues stood overgrown with ivy or sprawled in the long grass. But with a closer look, your blood would have run cold. For they were not statues, but the petrified, stony remains of unhappy travellers. Young men and old there were, pedlars and dukes: anyone unlucky enough to pass by Castle Pitiless and be seen by the Wicked Koschei. The castle was the sorcerer's evil lair, and his cruel magic stretched out from its walls in pools of black shadow. No matter where the sun stood in the sky, those shadows stretched to north, south, east and west.

There were no pretty girls among the statues. Koschei preferred simply to take girls prisoner and keep them captive in Castle Pitiless where he could enjoy looking at them. Like a cat watching goldfish in a pond.

One summer's day yet another young man strayed, unsuspecting, into the pretty wooded glade in Koschei's forest. He was Prince Ivan, separated from his fellow huntsmen and wandering lost among the trees, enjoying the birdsong.

All of a sudden, like fire from a dragon's mouth, a flash of orange streamed past his face. Then it was high above his head; next it was swooping through the long grass. A female bird the colour of flame, with streamers of fiery plumage, soared and tumbled between the branches, delighting in the warm sunshine. Ivan hid behind a tree so as not to scare her away.

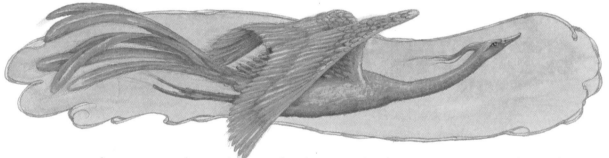

If ever good magic perched in an evil roost it was when the Firebird took her morning flight through the woods of Castle Pitiless. Prince Ivan gazed open-mouthed at her sheer speed and grace as she somersaulted through the sunbeams, filling her cloak of feathers with the gusting wind. Just for a moment she settled on the grass.

"Got you!" cried Prince Ivan, leaping out of his hiding place and wrapping both arms round her. "Wait till my friends see what I've caught on the hunt!" She struggled, but he held on tightly.

"No! No! Let me go! You must!" She twisted and writhed, but he would not free her. "If you have a drop of pity in you, sir, please don't cage me! I'll die if I can't fly in the open sky!"

Her tears alarmed him dreadfully. With one hand he smoothed her tousled plumage and with the other he set her down on her slender claws. "Shush! There, there! Calm yourself. Hush. Do you think I'd really keep hold of you if it meant harming you? I'm sorry. That's how we men are sometimes. When we see real beauty we can't help wanting to grab hold, to own it. I'm sorry to frighten you."

The Firebird trembled from head to foot, darted away to a safe distance, then stood looking at him. "You're a good, kind man. You won't be sorry you let me go. You think I'm weak, but I'm really quite powerful. Here. Have this." She plucked a scarlet feather from her breast and held it out to him. "If you ever need help, call me with this feather and I shall come in an instant." Then, with a flourish of her extraordinary wings, the Firebird soared into the air like the Phoenix which is born and reborn in a burst of flame.

She was no sooner gone than Prince Ivan heard voices – girls' voices – and another sudden flurry of colour burst into the clearing. He quickly hid again, to see what new wonders the wood had to offer.

But the girls who ran by were not like the Firebird. They were happy enough in their games and their dancing, but they were not free. Every time they looked back towards the castle, their faces grew sad. And each time they came across one of the stone statues, they flinched from it in horror.

One, the tallest, Ivan thought every bit as beautiful as the Firebird. He could not take his eyes off her. He left his hiding place just to see her better, and his heart burned as though the feather inside his jacket was truly a flicker of fire.

When the girls saw Ivan, they were startled and afraid. "Please don't run away! I won't hurt you," he said. And beckoning to one of them, he whispered, "Please won't you introduce me to that lady there – the one all in blue?"

"Princess Nadeshda, you mean?"

They barely needed an introduction. For the Princess was looking at Ivan much as he had looked at her. There was magic in that woodland glade, and not all of it was bad. The love between them was instant – like a lightning strike. But for the second time that day Prince Ivan found he could not take home with him the beauty he admired so much. "We are all prisoners of the evil sorcerer Koschei," explained the Princess. "He lets us out of . . . *that place* every day to breathe fresh air, but we can no more leave than if we were chained to the castle keep. This forest is just the pleasantest part of Koschei's prison . . . And you are inside it too, Ivan! Go now, before he sees you. Girls he keeps like castle pets, but men he turns to stone. See the statues? Now go! Forget me. Forget us all. Just go, before Koschei finds you. I couldn't bear it if you were to . . ."

A dismal bell began to toll inside Castle Pitiless, like the clang of a funeral knell. The girls at once began to move away, with slow, sad steps, looking back over their shoulders, powerless to stay. The iron gates in the wall swung shut behind them.

"No! Don't go!" Ivan begged, shaking at the gates with desperate hands. And the gates did indeed swing open again.

But this time it was not pretty girls who came out but demons, goblins, trolls and gremlins, beasts with furry jowls and piggy snouts, some with fangs, more with clawed paws snatching at Ivan's clothes and skin. They swept round him in a black flood, until he was marooned, cut off from all escape.

Then came Koschei – so huge he had to duck his head beneath the tree branches, and broke the mistletoe off the boughs. His long hair and beard were plaited with thorns, and his face was the colour of pestilence. "So! Another intruder, eh? Another trespasser! And what do we do with men who come where they're not invited?"

"*Turn them to stone! Turn them to stone!*" chanted his beastly, ferocious henchmen. "Do it, O master, for we love to sharpen our teeth on the Stone Ones and blunt our claws on them!"

"So be it!" cried Koschei. "Let him be turned to . . ."

Ivan did not know whether it was magic or fear that gripped his legs, that stole all the strength out of his arms. He felt an icy chill taking hold of him, of every part but one burning pool above his heart. It took all the strength he could muster to pull out the Firebird's feather and brandish it at Koschei.

"So soon?" came a cry from overhead. "Do you need my help so soon?" Down came the Firebird to stand beside him, her wings furling behind her like the folds of a streaming scarlet cloak.

"Oho! No grey stone death for *you*, my beauty!" laughed Koschei. "I shall put *you* in a cage and hang you in my window to sing for me!"

Then Prince Ivan regretted summoning the Firebird into such danger. For what could she do against so many terrible foes?

"Will you so?" said the Firebird, "And if I sing, will you dance?" Her wings cracked open like the panels of a kite.

All at once Koschei's demons began to shuffle about, then to shamble, with rolling shoulders and waving arms, in a kind of ugly jig. "*Dance*, Koschei!" commanded the Firebird, and even the giant ogre was powerless to disobey. His huge feet began to stamp, then to jump, then to skip crazily about, his big head lolling on his neck, and his hands shaking themselves loose at the ends of his arms. He hopped and jigged like a man overjoyed, but his face scowled and he yelled curses as the Firebird's magic forced him to dance on and on. She led the dancing, weaving in and out between the trees.

The goblins and ghouls, gremlins and demons groaned and moaned; their muscles ached, but their limbs would not let them rest. They sprang and vaulted over one another, begging their master to put a stop to their torment. They danced till the fur on their paws wore out. Koschei's shiny slippers flapped and scuffed, and the heels flew off in two different directions.

At last, when they were totally exhausted, the Firebird allowed them to rest. They dropped where they stood, panting and sobbing, and fell into an instant, snoring sleep. All but Koschei. He fell flat on his face, but his eyelids stayed open, watching. The Firebird herself showed not the smallest sign of weariness.

Ivan drew his hunting dagger and ran towards the sorcerer, swearing to kill him and put an end to all his filthy enchantments. The grisly ogre only bared his teeth in a spiteful grin.

"Can't kill me, pipsqueak," he panted. "I keep my soul in a safe place – outside my body – hidden away from fools like you."

Ivan turned to the Firebird for help, but it seemed she had no more magic to lend him. "Search out that soul, Ivan," she said. "Find it and destroy it. All his spells will be broken!" She spread her wings, preparing to leave. "I do remember, when I've flown through this wood before, seeing something round and white in the bole of a rotten tree . . . Goodbye now!"

His hand still raised in farewell, his thanks still echoing among the branches, Ivan started to search, racing from tree to tree. All the trunks looked green and sappy. Just one was black and blasted, as if lightning had struck it or poison crept up from the roots. In its hollow trunk lay a giant egg, white as a peeled snail, and about as heavy as a man's heart.

"Don't touch that! Let it alone! It's mine!" shrieked Koschei crawling towards Ivan, his bony fingers slashing the air.

But Ivan lifted the egg over his head and hurled it to the ground, shattering the shell. A yellow, sulphurous, stinking yolk spilled out and scorched the grass for ever. With a scream of despair, Koschei rolled over . . . and disappeared. His body, his wickedness and all his magic evaporated in a jet of purple smoke. When Ivan looked around, not a demon or a goblin was to be seen anywhere.

With a creak of unoiled hinges, the gates of Castle Pitiless swung open. The shadows falling to north, south, east and west melted away, and all the sweet prisoners inside came running out.

There, moving like someone in a dream, was Princess Nadeshda, dressed as a bride. But instead of a flower in her hands, she held a single bright feather. She too had been visited by the Firebird.

The girls brought Ivan wedding clothes, and coronets of flowers for him and his bride. "Stay and make a home in the castle, Prince. The sun shines in at the windows now. And there's a whole kingdom without a ruler. Be our King and Nadeshda can be our Queen, and it shall be called Castle Pitiless no longer, but Castle Ivan!"

So Ivan and Nadeshda became the rulers of that woodland kingdom. They renamed the castle 'Castle of the Firebird'. Often, around sunset, when the western sky turned red, a streak of scarlet flittered in and out of its turrets, making red glints in the windows, swooping down towards the river.

PETROUCHKA

Come with me to the Theatre of Life. Roll up! Roll up! Take your seat. The curtain will be rising soon on a snowy Russian scene filled with happy people. It's an old story, this one, set way back in old St Petersburg, one holiday in spring. It's a sad story, too, so don't forget: they are only actors playing out the plot. Just like puppets in a puppet theatre, really. Nothing to mind about.

One Shrove Tuesday, long ago, the square in old St Petersburg was alive with people all eager to spend their few kopeks having fun in the spring sunshine. There were stalls selling delicious pastries, sherbet powder, scalding tea; there were hooplas and coconut shies, fortune-tellers and pedlars.

Everyone began gathering in one spot. Not long now until the

puppet show. The old Puppet Master poked his icicle of a nose between the swagged curtains, inviting people to step closer and see the show.

When the curtains drew back, lifting their golden fringes off the plank stage, three puppets hung there, their strings looped about their drooping heads. But a quick drumroll, a squawk of trumpets, and they jerked into a dance as lively as any sailor's sweetheart or organ-grinder's daughter. There was a Saracen, huge and black, with a silver sabre sharp as a sickle moon, and his head swathed in a turban. He rolled a wicked pair of eyes towards the second puppet. Lyuba was such a pretty marionette, with long yellow hair and cornflower eyes and cheeks as red as blushes. She wore a belt studded with bells, and ballet shoes and dress fit for the Tsar's own daughter. Third and last was Little Peter – Petrouchka – a thin, wan clown in baggy pantaloons and a big ruffled collar. His face was deathly white and his mouth turned down so sadly that it made people laugh. It's odd that, isn't it? Year after year the audiences came to see him dance his sad little dances and laugh till the tears ran down their faces. Perhaps they were happy to see someone worse off than themselves.

If only they had known just how special Petrouchka was. For there was far more to him than a turned-down mouth and a baggy suit. Of all the puppets in the world, he had the most terrible secret. If eyes could have seen inside his canvas chest, his sawdust stuffing, they would have seen the glimmer of . . . a soul.

For by accident God had sewn a human soul into Peter's cloth chest, so that Peter felt what it was to love, as humans love. He loved Lyuba the Ballerina.

And she loved the Saracen.

Lyuba had no soul. She could not look inside another person's heart. She could only see the Saracen's big handsome body, his strong arms and leaping legs, those foreign eyes as they looked at her and smouldered. As the music played, the three puppets danced, with jerky movements, showing off what they could do.

Lyuba was laughing. She loved the big fellow paying her so much attention, showing off to her, chasing Peter away with that great shining sword. She liked Peter bringing her flowers too, of course, sighing and gazing. But, well, he was only Petrouchka, making an idiot of himself as usual. Nobody took him seriously.

That Shrove Tuesday Petrouchka tried to make her understand: how his love was something different – better – more real . . . human! But Lyuba had no eyes for him. She went on flirting with the Saracen.

"What's Peter doing? What's he playing at? He's attacking the Saracen, ha ha ha! He's *jealous*! Ha ha ha!"

"*Stop that!*" The Puppet Master's harsh voice startled everyone. He shook a bony fist, and at once the brawl on stage ended and the three puppets went back to dancing. Jig-jog, jig-jog. Knees bend, elbows out. One two three, in time to the music.

After the crowds had gone, the Puppet Master hurled the little clown into a poky room behind the stage and locked the door on him. Petrouchka pounded at the door, rattled the lock, but it was no good. He was shut up, all alone with his anger and despair. His human soul burned with anguish. He hated the Puppet Master and he loathed the Saracen with all the bitter scalding hatred of jealousy. He loved Lyuba with an aching, helpless passion. And now to be shut in! To be treated like a bunch of rags and kept from the cool evening air. He thought he would stifle.

"Peter! Oh, Petrouchka! Are you all right?"

"Lyuba!"

"Whatever got into you just now?" asked the pretty Ballerina, standing on tip-toe to speak through the window.

"Oh, I couldn't bear it, Lyuba! Not another minute! To see how that brute leers at you and paws at you and tries to kiss you. You shouldn't let him. You mustn't! You have me! Don't you know I've always loved you with a love that fairly rips my body to shreds?"

Lyuba stared at him with her big, empty blue eyes. "And who might you be to tell me who I can and can't dance with? Some little pasty-faced clown in baggy pants? Really!" And half in fright, half in temper, she ran away from the window.

No! Wait! Stop! Come back!" Little Peter wrenched at the door, hammered at the window and finally, in a frenzy of passion, hurled himself clear through the plywood wall of his back-stage prison. He knew exactly which way Lyuba had gone.

The Saracen might be a hulking, handsome bully but he was a

bit of a buffoon too. Between shows, lying about in his dressing room on sumptuous Arabian cushions and rugs, he had hardly a thought in his big empty head. As soon as she came prinking into his room, he wanted to cuddle and kiss her.

She was playing a little tin horn and flirting shamelessly, though a part of her was still wondering about Little Peter, so odd, so wild-eyed.

"Dance with me, my divine loveliness!" roared the Saracen . . . and Lyuba let herself be whirled about the room.

But soon she was tired of dancing and of having kisses planted in the nape of her neck and up and down her arms. "Stop now. Let go of me," she said, and when he did not, she grew quite alarmed and tried to pull away.

That was when Peter came rushing into the room. He kicked at the Saracen's legs, beat at the Saracen's broad back. He tried to prise open the strong, black fingers that gripped his beloved. But the Saracen only laughed, and threw Peter aside like a parcel of rags. Roaring like a bear, he drew his sword from its scabbard and sliced the air into shreds.

"Oh, do be careful, Peter! He'll kill you!" cried Lyuba, as the wicked blade whistled within a whisker of Peter's white face. There was no fighting such a man – Peter had no weapon. He was driven back and back, and finally sent running for his life.

Suddenly, scattering the crowds to right and left, the ghostly white figure of Little Peter came pelting through the fairground. His hair on end, his mouth a gaping, gasping O, his eyes like black holes torn in his white cloth face, he stumbled and tumbled in among the stalls and booths, looking for a hiding place.

The crowds did not know what to think. Was this some extra entertainment put on by the Puppet Master? They tittered nervously, and fell silent only when the Ballerina caught the Saracen up, dragged on his arm, hung on his clothing and begged, "Don't! Stop! No! Please! For my sake!"

The Saracen laughed. He barged through the crowd with his sword until he had cornered Peter against a high wall. "*No!*" screamed Lyuba.

With a thud and a rip of canvas, the curved scimitar struck, plunging deep into Peter's narrow chest. He slumped to the ground. The crowd pulled away in revulsion. Only Lyuba went to his side, tender and loving, to discover the truth: Peter was dead.

"Send for the police!" cried a woman in the crowd. "Murder! Murder!"

"Murder? Ha ha ha!" The Puppet Master's pointed hat shook with laughter. "A murder? Who do you think's been murdered, my dear lady?" He held up a small, ragged puppet, streams of sawdust trickling out through rents in its chest. "How can you *murder* a rag doll, eh? How can you kill a puppet? Ha ha ha!"

Then a noise pierced the night air so loud, so sharp, so eerie that all St Petersburg seemed to catch its breath. High above their heads, dancing on the wall, as fearless as any acrobat on a tightrope, a bright white form stretched its arms towards the sky.

"It's Petrouchka!"

"It's Little Peter!"

Lyuba looked up at him, one hand to her lips, one hand to her sawdust heart. "Oh, Peter! You're alive!"

And so he was, in a way. At least his happy soul was alive, freed to live on and leap up, as all human spirits are freed by death, to dance among the stars and the moons and the planets.

"It's a ghost come back to haunt me!" whimpered the cowardly, superstitious Saracen.

"He was just a puppet!" said the Puppet Master scornfully, doubtfully, trembling with terror. "How can a *puppet* haunt anyone?"

How indeed? Remember those words when you settle down in your seat and the curtains part and the Theatre of Life begins.

THE SLEEPING BEAUTY

A baby daughter was once born to a king and queen. She was more beautiful than most, more happy than many, more loved than all but you. Her mother and father wanted her to have everything in life, and what was there to prevent it? They were rich, lived in a splendid palace, and numbered among their friends all the fairies of the forest and field. Fairies with rainbow wings and dresses of gossamer danced at the christening, when the baby was named Aurora, 'the dawn', because she seemed like a promise of a wonderful day to come.

Well, in fact, one fairy was missing, but then Carabosse had disappeared from the country in a huff of temper and a puff of smoke, and had not been seen for years.

So the fairies danced around the cradle like wisps of colour weaving themselves into a rainbow. And they laid their wands on the sleeping child and blessed her with Beauty, Wealth, Joy, Love and Grace.

"*And I have a present for her too!*" cried a voice.

It was the Fairy Carabosse, quite scarlet with fury, her wings trembling with rage. "Here, Princess," she sneered, tossing like a curse a glittering gift into the cradle. "One day, show what promise you may, win what hearts you might, let *that* be the death of you! Prick your finger and die!"

The other fairies snatched the golden spindle out of the crib, as though it were a poisonous snake. They hurled it out of the window. They begged Carabosse to take back her fearful curse. But the evil-tempered, proud fairy was so offended at having been forgotten, overlooked, that no amount of tears could move her to pity.

"Then I must undo your mischief!" cried the Lilac Fairy, flittering from behind a curtain. "You thought your wicked gift was the last, but I still have mine to give! And though I can't undo your cruel magic, I can blunt its spiteful point. Let the Princess not die when she pricks her finger; let her sleep for a hundred years. Then, while she sleeps, let her blessings grow, so that she wakes to yet more joy than her friends can wish her today!"

Carabosse fumed and seethed. She stormed out, slamming the great doors with a noise that shook the very stones of the palace and the very hearts of the guests. But she was no sooner gone than she was forgotten, for the world has no wish to remember the wicked, only the good and the lovely.

Even so, King Floristan banished all spindles and spinning wheels from his kingdom, to make sure Princess Aurora could never prick her finger on one.

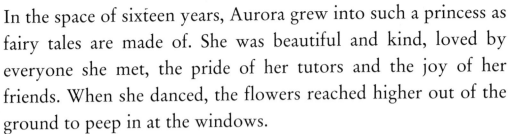

In the space of sixteen years, Aurora grew into such a princess as fairy tales are made of. She was beautiful and kind, loved by everyone she met, the pride of her tutors and the joy of her friends. When she danced, the flowers reached higher out of the ground to peep in at the windows.

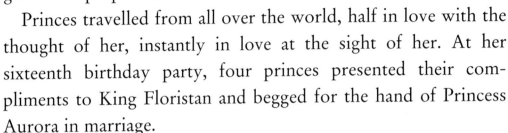

Princes travelled from all over the world, half in love with the thought of her, instantly in love at the sight of her. At her sixteenth birthday party, four princes presented their compliments to King Floristan and begged for the hand of Princess Aurora in marriage.

"You must ask her yourselves," said her parents. "We wouldn't choose to part with her for all the world, but it is time she spread happiness beyond the bounds of this small kingdom, and enjoyed the happiness of married life as well."

So the Prince of England and the Prince of Spain and the Prince of India and the Prince of France bowed low to the Princess Aurora and partnered her in the dancing. Each one thought he had won her heart.

"She smiled such a smile at me!"

"She held my hand so tenderly!"

"She danced as though her heart was on fire!"

"She laughed at *all* my jokes!"

And yet it was just Aurora's nature to make her friends and guests feel welcome. She was overbrimming with love – but not for any one man more than another.

So it was that she greeted the strange old woman shrouded in grey and cradling something in her arms. "A birthday present for you, my dear," croaked the old crone.

"Do I know you? How very kind. Every one has been so kind to me today," said Aurora. "What is it?"

About the size of a newborn baby, and almost as light, it was

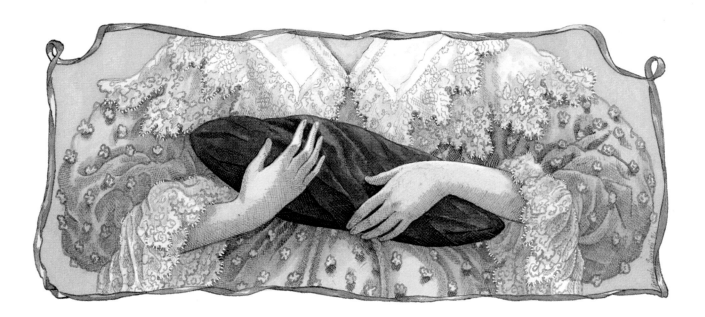

wrapped in cloth as black as spite. But as Aurora unwrapped it, the present glittered with the yellow of gold, the spangle of fleecy golden yarn, the silver sliver of a sharp needle. It was a spindle for spinning wool into yarn.

"Aurora, don't touch it!" cried her mother.

"Ow! Look, I've pricked my finger. You'd best take it from me. I shall put blood on the pretty wool."

Suddenly the room began to swim and melt, the floor to heave and the ceiling to bow.

"So tired," said Aurora, then fell flat, so deeply asleep that she did not even put out her hands to stop herself from falling.

"Carabosse, your spite has made you the shame of Fairyland. No tongue will ever speak to you again. No face will ever smile

your way. Leave here for ever." For a moment, Carabosse stood face to face with the Lilac Fairy, then, with a furious stamp of her foot, she was gone.

The King and Queen were sobbing; the Princes had all drawn their swords; Aurora's friends leaned over her, powerless to wake her. "Carry her to her bed!" commanded the Lilac Fairy. "Have you forgotten her fate? To sleep for one hundred years?"

"Then she might just as well be dead, for we shall never see her dance or smile again," sobbed the King. "We shall all be dead long since when she opens her eyes again."

But it was not the Lilac Fairy's intention to keep only Aurora safe, swaddled in dreamless sleep. She swept her wand over the heads of the courtiers and ladies-in-waiting, the princes and guests, the King and Queen. And one by one they fell asleep where they stood or sat or sprawled or knelt, sinking into sleep like the leaves settling to the ground from an autumn tree.

And as the Court of King Floristan sank down, up sprang a

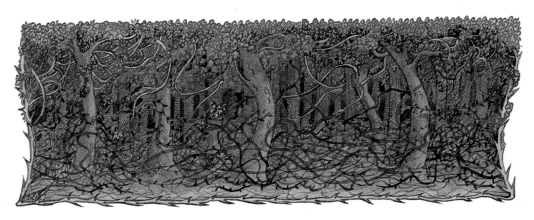

hedge round his palace; trees and brambles and briars and bushes conjured out of the ground by the Lilac Fairy's wand. They buried the palace steps, they smothered the palace windows, they muffled its high turrets. The topmost branches stretched protective twigs over the tiled roofs, so that the entire building was smothered in creepers and thorns. So dense was the greenery that a stranger riding by might see no palace there at all.

Of course the people who lived in the villages near by knew of the palace, knew that their king and queen and princess were lost somewhere inside the magic barricade of trees. At first they talked of nothing else. The wonder of it filled their every thought. They tried to get in – failed every time – said the thorns were sharp as needles, the creepers unbreakable.

But there were pigs to feed, the corn to be cut, the sheep to shear, the roof to patch. And people forget the most marvellous things after a few busy years. Those who had ever seen King Floristan, his courtiers and his lovely daughter grew old and died.

After sixty or seventy years the palace in the wood was only a rumour, a legend, a fairy story half believed, about a sleeping beauty and a magic spell.

Exactly one hundred years after Aurora's sixteenth birthday, a young prince called Charmant rode by on the highway with his friends. The forest seemed a pleasant place for a picnic. There was a sudden flicker of movement among the trees.

"A deer!" cried the Prince's aide. "Let's hunt it!"

The others were eager enough, but somehow Prince Charmant had no taste for the hunt. When his friends all rushed away into the tangled undergrowth, he remained behind. "What is this place?" he wanted to know. "Why does it give me such a strange feeling? Why does it make my heart beat faster?"

"They say there is a palace in the heart of the forest," said a voice.

"Who are you? Where did you come from? I didn't see you before."

"And at the heart of the palace a room," said the girl in the lilac dress. "And at the heart of the room a bed."

"And at the heart of the bed?"

"A beautiful princess. Sleeping."

The Prince leapt up and rushed at the wall of dense green: knotted creepers, tangles of thorn, fallen branches, barricades of tree trunks and, underfoot, slippery moss. "Do you know these parts? Can you show me a way through? Is there a way through?" he begged to know.

"For you? Oh yes. I believe so," said the girl in lilac, and idly breaking off a wand of grass crowned with a star of thistledown she began to pick her way through the tangled undergrowth. Charmant kept close, following in her footsteps. And strangely

enough, the thorns (though they were sharp as needles) never once snagged her lilac dress, nor scratched his own face or hands.

Suddenly his boots stumbled against steps, steps rising upwards to the mossy splendour of an arched doorway. No lock kept him out. No guard challenged him. All the candles had burned down to their holders. All the firegrates were snowy with ash.

In every doorway, passageway and chair, people lay fast asleep. But the girl in lilac did not seem to think them important, for she

led him onwards to a bedroom in the heart of the palace. There, in the heart of a snowy bed, untouched by cobwebs, lay a young girl. She was dressed in her finest clothes, as if for a party, and her beautiful face was tilted upwards as if awaiting a kiss.

Strange, to kiss a stranger, especially a stranger lying unconscious in an enchanted palace. And yet he could not help it. It seemed as if Charmant's whole life had been one long wait for this particular day, for this particular kiss.

As their lips touched, her eyes flew open, and his fate was sealed. Beautiful in her sleep, his Sleeping Beauty was still more lovely half awake.

She stirred. She sat up. She put her feet gingerly to the ground and looked around, puzzled at finding herself so far from the party. And yet she did not look around as much as she might, for she could hardly bear to look away from the face of Prince Charmant. Had he kissed her? What a saucy liberty to take, uninvited! And yet she thought her heart would burst if he did not kiss her again.

Throughout the palace, courtiers and ladies-in-waiting

stretched and yawned, rubbed stiff necks, puzzled at how they could possibly have fallen asleep at the height of the birthday party. Then they remembered. The King and Queen hugged one another as they remembered. It was a strange feeling to go to sleep and wake up one hundred years later.

"Am I old and hideous?" asked the Queen.

"Not a day older than . . . than . . . than when I last saw you," said the King. "Not one hour. Not one minute."

The orchestra began to pluck their instruments – and found them still in tune, even after a century's silence.

The spell was broken. The trees melted away from round the

palace like clematis dying back for the winter months. The thorns melted like spiky frost. The dense leaves flew away like a flock of a million green birds, into a cloudless sky.

All the fairies in Fairyland were invited to the wedding, just as they had been to the christening. Even Carabosse was invited, to see how her evil had been turned to good. But though a herald searched the whole kingdom and far beyond, there was no trace of Carabosse – only a few bitter aloes growing where her gossamer hammock had once hung.

And what more natural at a wedding blessed by fairies, than that the characters of fairy tales should come along as guests: Tom Thumb, Puss in Boots, Red Riding Hood, Beauty and her Beast. After the ceremony and the dancing, these famous celebrities told their stories as the new candles glimmered in a thousand candelabras, and the wedding guests listened, entranced. Only Aurora and her Prince Charmant remained dancing, held in Love's spell for evermore.